Then his lips
and firm and
late, and she

He'd kissed her like this five years ago, and
her heart had felt giddy for a week…

For a moment nothing else happened, but then
he moved, just slightly, tilting his head and
placing tiny nibbling kisses all across her
mouth and chin, and she felt a shiver of
something unfamiliar and wonderful race
through her veins. He'd never kissed her
like this!

Caroline Anderson's nursing career was brought to an abrupt halt by a back injury, but her interest in medical things led her to work first as a medical secretary and then, after completing her teacher training, as a lecturer in Medical Office Practice to trainee medical secretaries. She lives in rural Suffolk with her husband, two daughters and assorted animals.

Recent titles by the same author:

MAKING MEMORIES
THE GIRL NEXT DOOR
PRACTICALLY PERFECT
AN UNEXPECTED BONUS

JUST A
FAMILY DOCTOR

BY
CAROLINE ANDERSON

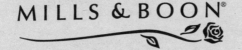

MILLS & BOON®

First published in Great Britain 2000
Harlequin Mills & Boon Limited,
Eton House, 18-24 Paradise Road, Richmond, Surrey TW9 1SR

© Caroline Anderson 2000

ISBN 0 263 82263 X

Set in Times Roman 10½ on 12 pt.
03-0010-50005

Printed and bound in Spain
by Litografia Rosés, S.A., Barcelona

CHAPTER ONE

ALLIE heard a soft footfall behind her. 'There you are,' she said. 'I thought you were never coming. Anna, we're going to have to get this rota sorted out—I need the weekend of the—ah!'

Her hands flew up and grasped the fingers covering her eyes—firm, masculine fingers, strong and unyielding and attached to someone with a sexy chuckle and a wicked sense of humour.

'Guess who?' a voice said, and she stopped struggling instantly, all her senses leaping to attention. The voice sounded strangely familiar. It couldn't be—could it?

'Mark?' she said incredulously, and the hands fell away, releasing her.

'Damn. You guessed.'

She leapt up and spun round, and laughter bubbled up inside her. 'It *is* you!' she exclaimed, and found herself wrapped in a huge hug. She indulged herself for a moment, then pushed away, looking up at him with laughing eyes, scanning his face in delight. 'You sneaky rat! And how did you know where I was—did my mother tell you?'

The answering smile was swift and wide, lighting his gorgeous grey eyes and crinkling them at the corners. He looked good enough to eat, but then he always had. 'I'm afraid so,' he confessed.

'So, what are you doing here?' she asked in amazement.

'I've come to say happy birthday,' he said with a grin.

'What—all the way from London?'

He chuckled. 'No. Actually, all the way from Andrew Barrett's clinic. I'm working here—doing a paediatric rotation. I started today.'

'Really? That's amazing, we'll be working together! Oh, Mark, that's wonderful! I haven't seen you for such a long time—'

'Five years.'

'Is it really?' she said in amazement. 'I suppose it must be—I was nearly eighteen, and I'm twenty-three today. Oh, Mark, it's really good to see you again. We ought to catch up—lunch? Oh, damn, no, I can't do lunch, I'm meeting my housemates for a drink. You could come?' she suggested doubtfully.

'I'd rather have you to myself—it's difficult to catch up in a crowd. How about tonight? Are you going out?'

'No—I'm not. Beth and Lucy were both busy tonight—that's why we're having lunch.'

'No hot date?'

'No date at all, hot or otherwise,' she said with a wry chuckle. 'Tonight would be lovely.'

'Where do you live?'

'Just behind the hospital in a little terraced house. Where are you?'

'I've got a room in the hospital—one of those ghastly things like university halls. It could be worse, I suppose. It's got an *en suite* shower room and trees outside the window, but it's pretty grim.'

'You ought to get a flat.'

'I'm hoping to buy a house—I just need time to look. I've got my next job lined up in the same area, so I thought I'd buy now. Why not? The sooner the better, frankly, after last night. Talk about rowdy.'

'You're getting too old,' she teased, and he laughed.

'Tell me about it.' He glanced at his watch and sighed. 'Listen, I have to fly. I just wangled ten minutes and I've already been gone fifteen. How about meeting me at seven at the back entrance by the accommodation block?'

'Sure. I'll look forward to it. Where are we going?'

He shrugged. 'Search me. I only arrived in this town last night. You choose—I'll do as I'm told.'

'OK. See you later.'

'Sure.'

He waggled his fingers, whipped the door open and strode down the ward, leaving her staring after him with a daft smile on her face.

'Who was that?'

She looked at Anna, watching Mark's retreat with undisguised curiosity, and laughed. 'An old friend. Mark Jarvis—he's doing a paeds rotation. He just came to say happy birthday.'

'It's your birthday?'

'Yup—and I get to do Darren's colostomy pouch, just to celebrate. Want to help?'

Anna laughed. 'I'll come and cheerlead. So, tell me how you know that gorgeous hunk, you lucky girl!'

She shrugged. 'He stayed with us five years ago and spent a couple of weeks with my father while he was doing his clinical-GP work experience.'

'So you don't know anything else about him? Like if he's married or whatever?'

Was Anna really interested in him? Good heavens!

What a thought—and a strangely disturbing one, at that...

'I don't know anything about him any more,' she said, and realised that it was utterly true. She knew nothing, other than that he'd been a charming and delightful house guest, her mother had adored him, her father had thought he was excellent doctor material, and she—well, the less she thought about that, the longer her sanity might remain intact!

'I'll have to get my sleuths out,' Anna mused. 'Unless you want the first option on him?'

Allie laughed. 'I don't think so. I don't think he's interested—not like that. He certainly wasn't then.'

The thought was curiously disappointing.

Mark strode along the corridor towards A&E, whistling softly under his breath and conscious of the smile that lingered round his eyes. Allie Baker, all grown up and even more gorgeous. Whoever would have thought it?

He wondered idly if she was involved with anyone at the moment. Her mother hadn't been specific, and he hadn't liked to ask her. Still, she didn't have a date tonight, so maybe that was hopeful.

He turned the corner, pushed the door out of the way and headed for the work station in the centre of the busy A&E department.

'Hi, I'm Mark Jarvis, paediatric SHO. I believe you wanted me?'

The nurse looked up and smiled. 'Oh, hi. Yes, we've got a youngster with a classic appendix. Can you admit her and let the surgical team know?'

He gave a wry grin. 'I can try. I've only just joined the department this morning. I'm not much of a paediatrician yet, I'm afraid, and as for the hospital routine—!'

She slid off her stool and returned the grin. 'Come on, I'll talk you through it.'

It was simple enough, once he'd learned the way things were done at the Audley Memorial. Not so very different from any of the other hospitals he'd been at recently while he'd worked his way through his house years. Surgery first, mainly, then a host of other short rotations, covering all the various aspects of medicine that would be useful to him when he did his training as a GP registrar in a few months' time.

Of course it would have been quicker if he'd known straight away what branch he wanted to specialise in, but he'd been all round the houses before he'd finally made up his mind that general practice and not surgery was the job for him, and he supposed it was all useful experience.

However, the fragmented, nomadic lifestyle dictated by the last few years was very unsettling. It would be wonderful, he thought with an inward sigh, to settle down in one place and learn a routine that was going to last him longer than three or six months!

The nurse was right, it was a classic appendix, and he admitted the child to the ward pending her operation, and went back up to find that Allie was nowhere in sight and the redhead in the sister's uniform was giving him considering looks. *Those* kind of looks. Oops. He hoped she wasn't going to be a problem, because he and Allie had unfinished business.

Well, he did, at any rate. The same might not be true of Allie, of course. The first thing he had to do was find out if she was seeing someone. Anything was possible, even if she didn't have a date on her birthday—

'Hi, I'm Anna Long, and you're Dr Jarvis. We haven't met. How are you getting on?' the Sister asked him with a direct and challenging smile.

'Fine—another routine to learn, but I expect I'll cope. I'm Mark, by the way.'

Anna smiled again, and he looked around. 'Is the girl from A&E with appendicitis here yet?'

'On her way. Allie's just getting her bed ready with another nurse.' She shot him a sidelong glance. 'I gather you and Allie know each other?'

He nodded, wondering what was behind those innocent eyes. Maybe nothing. 'Yes. I stayed with her parents for a couple of weeks several years ago. I haven't seen her since. Lots of catching up to do.'

Anna nodded, and he wondered if he was flattering himself or if that was something akin to disappointment that flickered in her eyes. Probably his imagination.

The child with appendicitis arrived, and he did all her paperwork and talked to her parents, and the surgical registrar arrived and checked her over and told them she'd be going up to Theatre in a little while.

Mark ordered a top-up of pain relief should it be necessary, and then as he was about to leave her bedside he caught a flash of pale gold hair as Allie bustled past. He excused himself and followed her.

'Allie.'

She jumped and turned round, hand on heart. 'You frightened the life out of me!' she said with a laugh. 'How's our new patient?'

'Fine. Well, she's not fine, but she will be. She's off to Theatre soon. I've done all the paperwork. I

CAROLINE ANDERSON

have to see a young lad with a colostomy—Darren someone?'

'Forsey. He's in the single room here. Can you manage?'

He laughed softly. 'I expect so. Are you busy?'

She nodded, then glanced at her watch. 'I'm always busy. I have to fly—I've got loads to do. I'll see you at seven if not before.'

'OK.' He watched her go, watched the sway of her hips that even the hopelessly unflattering uniform couldn't render sexless, and felt the tug of an old and familiar desire. Seven o'clock seemed a long time away...

She must be crazy. If only they'd been able to manage lunch it wouldn't have seemed so much like a date, but she'd promised to meet Lucy and Beth, her housemates, because they were on duty until late tonight and then Lucy had a meeting, and they'd wanted to celebrate her birthday.

Lunch would have been so much better. He just wanted a chat, and now she'd booked a table at a little bistro round the corner, and she was having serious doubts over whether it was too smart or if he'd just meant some pub for a quick drink and a packet of crisps!

Oh, well, she'd go halves. It didn't matter, she had nothing else to spend her money on and it would be nice to go out for dinner for a change. If only she didn't have this little fizzle in the pit of her stomach. She hoped she wasn't going down with something, but she did feel strange.

Excited, almost—

She stabbed her eye with the mascara wand and

growled at herself. Excited? He wasn't interested in her—and she wasn't interested in him any longer—was she?

Black tears streamed down her cheek, and she blotted and patched and gave up. It was dark outside, and the light in the bistro was pretty lousy. He wouldn't even notice, and it didn't matter if he did.

She slipped into her coat and shoes, pocketed her house keys and went out into the crisply chilly night. It was just a short walk over to the hospital, and it was well lit, but it still gave her the creeps. You never knew when a weirdo would be hanging around, and they found out where the nurses lived and put pressure on them for drugs and needles and so on.

It could be dangerous, but that was one of the hazards of living outside the hospital, and she'd had her fill of institutional living. She crossed the road, went through the gate past Security and reached the door just as Mark emerged.

'Perfect timing,' she said brightly, and wondered if her heart was going to crash against her ribs *every* time she clapped eyes on him, or only for the first few days—or weeks—or months!

Darn it. That fizzle was back!

His smile lit the gloomy area behind the building, and warmed her against the chilling wind. 'My car's over here, or are we walking?'

'Oh, we can walk, it's only round the corner and parking's difficult there,' she said. 'I've booked a table at a little bistro—it's very reasonable, and it's quite nice, unless you wanted to go to a pub somewhere?'

'No, not at all. A bistro sounds lovely. I'm starving.'

They strode briskly out along the pavement, huddled up against the bite of the wind. It made conversation difficult, and they hardly talked until they arrived at the restaurant. Then Mark settled back in his chair, hands in his pockets and looking altogether too luscious for her peace of mind, and grinned. 'So—tell me all about yourself. How long have you been qualified? A year? Two?'

'A year, just,' she told him. 'What about you? You must be twenty-seven now—quite the old man!'

He chuckled. 'That's right. It was a long time ago, wasn't it?' His eyes smiled, and she wondered what he was remembering. 'So, what have you been doing with yourself?' he asked, leaning forwards and toying with a breadstick.

'Apart from finishing my A levels, and training as a paediatric nurse? Not a lot.'

'So you're not married.'

She shook her head. 'No—no, I'm not married, or anything like that. Just me, on my own. Well, not really on my own. I've got two housemates, but they're both nurses and work odd hours, so there's usually only one there at the most at any given moment. What about you?' she asked, suddenly conscious of the importance of his answer. 'Are you married?'

He smiled and leant back again, crunching the breadstick thoughtfully. 'No, I'm not married—or anything like that—either. Just me, on my own, like you.'

She felt a sudden and absurd little rush of relief that she didn't care to analyse. 'So how's the career going?' she added, struggling for less rivetingly personal conversation. 'Still headed for general surgery?'

'Well, actually—'

'Good evening, sir, madam. Are you ready to order?'

She looked up at the waiter and smiled. 'I don't know. What's the chef's special tonight? It's normally very good.'

'Tagliatelle carbonara,' he said with pride. 'It's superb! Rich and creamy, the sauce is wonderful, with a fresh, crisp side salad.' He kissed his fingers expressively. 'Trust me, you'll love it, madam.'

She laughed. 'You've sold it to me. I'll have it, it sounds good.'

'Sir?'

Mark closed the menu. 'Sounds excellent. And a bottle of house red—is red OK for you, Allie?'

She nodded. 'Lovely. Thanks.'

He leant back, toying with another breadstick. 'So, tell me about your parents,' he said. 'Are they still well? I spoke to them briefly the other day, but I'm afraid I've been a bit lax about keeping in touch.'

'They're fine. My father's taking early retirement—the strain of general practice. He's nearly fifty-five, and he's stopping after Christmas. He says they're going to have lots of holidays, but I'm worried about him. I think he's suffering from stress, or maybe there's something else—perhaps something he won't tell us. I mean, why else would he give up so early?'

Mark laughed softly. 'Early? Fifty-five? My father died at fifty-eight. He'd planned early retirement and then changed his mind. If he'd taken it, he might still be alive. Anyway, you said your father looks well.'

'Oh, he is,' she admitted, wondering if she was just worrying unnecessarily, being a fussy daughter like he'd been a fussy parent. Who could tell? 'I'm sorry about your father. It must have been awful—Mum wrote and told me, but I didn't have your address so I didn't get in touch. Was it very sudden?'

'Pretty much. It was his heart—he thought he'd got indigestion. He was a doctor, for God's sake. He should have known better.'

The waiter arrived, whisking the plates onto the table in front of them with a flourish and bidding them to enjoy their meal. It broke the sombre thread of their conversation, and as they ate she told him a little about her job at the hospital and what it was like on the paediatric ward.

'It's a good hospital, I like it here,' she told him, twirling tagliatelle on her fork and licking sauce off her lips.

Mark was doing the same, and her eyes were suddenly riveted to the tip of his tongue as it chased a drop of sauce across that firm, chiselled lower lip. Desire, hot and swift and unfamiliar, hit her in the solar plexus like a blow from a sledgehammer.

'Food's pretty good,' he commented between mouthfuls, and she dragged in a lungful of air and smiled.

'Good. I'm glad you like it.'

Her phone rang, saving her from the impossible task of conversing intelligently when her body was suddenly hell-bent on betraying her. Had he been as stunningly attractive as this before? 'Excuse me,' she muttered, and dived into her bag, coming up with the little mobile handset. 'Hello?'

'Darling, happy birthday,' her mother said. 'Had a good day? I tried you at the house but you're obviously out. Anywhere nice?'

She met Mark's eyes and smiled. 'Actually, yes,

I'm sitting in a bistro with Mark Jarvis—you are a sneaky woman,' she told her mother laughingly. 'I'll call you later, we're in the middle of eating.' She slipped the phone back into her handbag and looked at Mark.

'By the way, this was my idea so we're going halves,' she told him.

He snorted. 'I don't think so. I seem to remember it was my idea.'

'I suggested we got together—'

'And I said how about tonight. My idea.'

'But I made the reservation—'

'And displayed excellent taste. Well done. It's still my treat.'

Allie rolled her eyes and laughed. 'Look, fair's fair—'

'You know what? You're too darned independent,' he said with a smile. 'If I want to take you out and spoil you, I will. What's wrong with that?'

She sighed. 'Nothing, so long as you don't get carried away—'

'Sounds fascinating,' he said in that husky, sexy, chocolate voice. 'When shall we start?'

She laughed and slapped his hand as he reached for another breadstick, and he grinned and snapped a bit off and fed it to her. 'Happy birthday, Allie,' he said softly, and she nearly choked on it.

Those eyes...!

He paid for the meal—of course! They lingered over dessert, a sinful chocolate confection with lashings of cream and something distinctly alcoholic lurking at the bottom of the dish, and then had a brandy and wonderful rich, dark coffee with mints while they

talked about the hospital and she told him what she
knew about the staff.

'I have a feeling Anna's on the prowl,' he commented, peeling another wafer-thin mint out of its little wrapper and feeding it to her.

Feeling decadent and a little tipsy, she took it with
her teeth and met his eyes, and felt a jolt of desire
like electricity course through her. Was he interested
in Anna? Was he pumping her? Damn—

'Anna?' she murmured, and cleared her throat.
'Um—possibly. She was asking about you.'

He arched an enquiring brow. 'And what did you
tell her?'

'Nothing. I said I knew nothing. It's true. I don't
know you at all.' More's the pity.

His smile held a promise that made her feel giddy.
'We'll have to do something about that,' he said
lightly. He looked around and caught the waiter's eye.
'Could we have our bill please—unless you want anything else?'

She shook her head and grinned. 'Oh, no, I've had
more than enough. I couldn't eat or drink another
thing.'

He paid the bill with a credit card, and then he
helped her into her coat, his hands settling it on her
shoulders with a gentle squeeze. He turned the collar
up and snuggled her down into the neck, and then
tugged on his own coat and buttoned it before opening the door and ushering her out into the night.

It was crisp and bright, but the wind had dropped
and it felt strangely warmer. They strolled this time,
arm in arm, unhurried, back through the dimly lit
streets behind the hospital. When they were almost
there, he hesitated. 'Where do you live? I'll walk you

home. I can't have you wandering about at this time of night by yourself.'

'What about you?' she said sensibly. 'You could be mugged or stabbed just as easily.'

He chuckled. 'Not quite, I don't think. I must weigh five stone more than you, for a start.'

She snorted. 'I doubt it. Three, perhaps, but never five.'

'Semantics. I'm bigger, I'm tougher and I'm probably a darn sight meaner than you are.'

She smiled and gave up. 'Whatever. It's down here.'

She led him to her front door, and he paused there, looking down at her in the shadow of the porch. 'There. Safely home,' he said.

There was a pause, an infinitesimal hesitation, and anticipation tiptoed over her skin.

'Thank you so much for a lovely evening,' she said softly. 'It's been wonderful.'

'Good,' he said, but still he didn't move.

Instead he stood there, staring down into her eyes, and when she thought she'd scream from the suspense he smiled slightly. 'I can't let you go without a birthday kiss,' he murmured, and his head lowered, blotting out the yellow glow from the streetlight.

Then his lips touched hers, warm and firm and traced with chocolate, and she nearly smiled. He'd kissed her like this five years ago, and her heart had felt giddy for a week...

For a moment nothing else happened, but then he moved, just slightly, tilting his head and placing tiny nibbling kisses all across her mouth and chin, and she felt a shiver of something unfamiliar and wonderful race through her veins. He'd never kissed her like this!

A tiny noise erupted from her lips, too small to be a whimper, but he heard it, and with a groan he eased her closer, wrapped his arms firmly round her and plundered her mouth with his.

He tasted of chocolate and coffee, with a trace of brandy, and it was enough to intoxicate her already fuddled brain. Without a care, without a modest thought or a second's pause, she slipped her arms around his neck, tilted her head and kissed him right back.

It felt wonderful. His tongue was like rough velvet, probing and caressing, seeking out the hidden recesses of her mouth and tormenting them with his touch. Their tongues played tag, chasing and retreating, and when after an age he lifted his head, he was breathing hard and a smile lurked in his eyes.

'Wow,' he murmured.

She laughed softly and said, 'Wow, indeed.'

He hugged her, tucking her head under his chin and holding her close, and she could feel the rise and fall of his chest against her cheek.

'Sorry, that was five years of curiosity coming to the fore,' he murmured against her hair.

'What?' She tipped back her head and searched his face. 'What do you mean?'

He gave a wry grin. 'Just that I've wondered for the last five years what it would be like to kiss you— really kiss you, not just that little kiss goodbye, but a real, honest-to-goodness proper kiss.'

'You didn't notice me!' she protested.

'No—I tried to ignore you. There's a difference. You were my host's daughter. You were seventeen, totally innocent and much too sweet for what I had in mind.'

'I had spots and puppy fat,' she said bluntly.

He chuckled. 'Rubbish. You were lovely. You were just young, and I was a guest in your parents' house.'

'And now?' she asked without pausing to think of the consequences.

His smile softened. 'Now I think we're on the same playing field. We're both adults, we're both available—why not just see what happens?'

Excitement tingled along her veins, and her legs threatened to give way. Astonishingly, she was speechless.

He bent his head and kissed her again, just lightly, and then winked. 'Go on, go inside before I change my mind and forget I'm supposed to be a gentleman.'

She was almost tempted, but a belated sense of propriety prevailed and she slipped her key in the lock, twisted it and opened the door.

'Goodnight, Mark—and thank you for a lovely evening.'

'My pleasure. Happy birthday.'

And, blowing her a kiss, he turned on his heel and strode up the path and across the street towards the hospital.

When he was out of sight she closed the door, sagged back against it and sighed luxuriously.

'That was a tender farewell,' Lucy said, whipping open the sitting room door just next to her.

She felt colour scorch her cheeks. 'Are you spying on me?' she demanded laughingly.

'No—should I have been? What did I miss?'

'A real treat,' Beth said, following Lucy out into

the hall. 'I just watched him walk down the road—
wow. Where on earth did he come from?'

Allie gave an embarrassed laugh. 'I've known him
for years. He did some work experience with my father five years ago.'

'He was a well-kept secret,' Lucy grumbled, trail-
ing into the kitchen.

'He wasn't a secret—I haven't seen him since, until
today. He just turned up on the ward.'

'And romance blossomed! How wonderful!'

'Beth, you have a vivid imagination.'

'Is that why you've got whisker burn on your top
lip?' she said mildly.

Allie's hand flew up to investigate, and they
laughed at her, the teasing, kindly laughter of good
friends. 'Go for it, kid,' Lucy said sagely. 'It's about
time.'

It probably was, she acknowledged as she went up
to bed, a steaming mug of tea in hand. She was
twenty-three, a professional woman on the threshold
of her career, and untouched by human hand. It hadn't
really been deliberate, except that she was naturally
fastidious and had heard such awful stories from her
friends that she'd never felt inclined to dabble or ex-
periment, and nobody had come along who'd pushed
her buttons.

Nobody except Mark, that is, but he'd been out of
reach and a hero figure at a most impressionable time.
The trouble was, the impression had been lasting, and
despite a few relationships with young men during
her training, the affection she'd felt for them had
never been enough for her to take that next and most
intimate step.

The memory of his farewell kiss as he was leaving

all those years ago had haunted her, and nothing else had measured up. *Nobody* else. As an adolescent she'd wanted the touch of Mark's hand, the feel of his lips, the warmth of his body. Apparently she still did.

She felt the soft, bruised skin of her lips and remembered the kiss they'd just shared, and a deep yearning ache flared to life within her. She'd been subconsciously waiting for him so long—would it be worth waiting for? Was it possible she'd find the love she needed in her life with Mark, or was it just wishful thinking?

She seen her friends flit from one man to another, unfulfilled and often desperately unhappy, and she didn't want that for herself. When she gave herself, it would be for ever. Did Mark feel the same? They might be on the same playing field now in terms of age, but was it a level playing field in terms of expectations, or was she going to open herself up to heartbreak if she allowed them to see what happened, as he suggested?

'Oh, for heaven's sake!' she grumbled, putting her tea down and pulling off her clothes. 'You went out for a cheap meal to a basic little Italian. You're making much too much of it, building too much on such a slight acquaintance. You don't even know the man.'

But she wanted to, and that was scary. She hadn't felt like this before, not since—well, not since they'd first met and they'd sat for hours talking, night after night. They'd talked about everything—religion, politics, music, medical ethics, the fact that her father wanted her to be a doctor and she wanted to be a nurse.

He'd supported her, talking through it with her, giving her a very sane piece of advice.

'Be true to yourself,' he'd said. 'You have to do that. If you aren't true to yourself, you can't be true to anyone else, because everything else is built on a lie.'

It had given her the courage to talk to her father, to explain that being clever enough to be a doctor didn't mean it was the career she wanted. Her mother had understood, but then her mother had been a nurse. And gradually, over the next few weeks, her father had come to understand—all thanks to Mark.

She owed him so much for that. She'd never thought she'd see him again, but now he was back in her life, and she realised she wanted to know much more about him—his likes and dislikes, his taste in music, his preferences in literature—all the things she hadn't had time to find out before. Suddenly it seemed very important. She had felt happier tonight in his company than she'd felt in five years.

Please God, let him feel the same, she thought as she curled up in bed with her tea. Don't let it be one-sided. Give us a chance. Let it be for real...

CHAPTER TWO

THE ward was busy the next morning when she arrived for work at seven. She'd thought she wouldn't sleep, but in fact had gone out like a light when her head hit the pillow. That's what happiness does for you, she'd told herself as she scrabbled around getting ready in a hurry. Or, more likely, half a bottle of red wine, a brandy and that sinfully laced chocolate dessert!

She had arrived in the nick of time, and found the night staff getting the children ready for their breakfast. There was always a flurry of visits to the loo and a rush round with bedpans to the immobile patients at that time of the morning, and Allie was as busy as any of them.

Anna was there, taking report from the Night Sister, and the moment it was done she joined Allie in the little single room where she was replacing Darren's colostomy pouch.

The twelve-year-old had come in with a rectal abscess, with fever and severe pain, following chronic constipation and an appalling diet, and after investigation they had decided to operate. The surgeons had cut through his bowel above the abscess and brought the cut end out through the wall of his abdomen in a temporary colostomy, to rest the affected area and allow it to heal, and for the next few weeks at least he would have to tolerate the indignity of a bag stuck on the front of his tummy.

Still, at least it wasn't permanent, Allie thought, carefully peeling the old bag away and sealing it and throwing Anna a smile at the same time.

'Morning.'

'Morning. Hi, Darren, how're you doing?' Anna asked, and chatted for a moment to him, then perched on the end of the bed and watched Allie work. 'A little bird tells me you went out for dinner with Mark last night, you sly old fox,' she murmured.

Allie felt a rush of guilt, then stifled it. I got there first, she told herself—five years ago! 'Not really dinner,' she denied, still not sure exactly what had happened. 'We went to the bistro—it was my birthday. Can you hold your T-shirt up higher for me, Darren? That's lovely. Thanks.'

'And did you bring cream cakes in?' Anna prodded, clearly feeling no malice towards Allie for having stolen the brightest prospect on the ward for years. 'No, you didn't. I hope you've brought them today.'

Allie smiled ruefully. 'Sorry. I haven't had time to get to the bakery—anyway, cream cakes are fattening, isn't that right, Darren?'

'Yeah—and I can't have one, so you can't either.'

'No, you can't, but we could always save you one for later—we need any excuse we can get for a cream cake at coffee time!' She propped herself on the edge of the treatment couch and grinned at the patient. 'We all need treats, don't we, Darren?'

Darren nodded. 'I fancy a cream cake. I'm bored with eating nothing decent. Can't you sneak off to the bakery now?'

'No—and anyway, you know you can't have a cream cake,' Allie told him with mock sternness. 'You need to rest your stomach for a few more days, not overload it with junk food, and besides, it's not my birthday any more.'

'We could pretend.'

'No, we couldn't. It's too soon after your operation.'

He poked his tongue out, and Allie chuckled and pressed the new pouch firmly in place. 'We'll pretend when you're better. There. That's you sorted. I'll come and see you in a while—unless you want to go into the playroom and watch telly with the others?'

He shook his head. 'Not yet. Perhaps tomorrow.'

'OK.' She smiled and gave him a quick hug, then pushed the trolley back to the treatment room and cleared up the equipment. 'He hates it,' she murmured to Anna as she worked.

'I know. It must be hell on a kid to have a colostomy, even if it's only temporary. Let's just hope the abscess clears up quickly.'

'Absolutely—but at least he's not in so much pain now. He just needs to heal and learn to eat the right foods—and definitely no cream cakes, no matter how bored he is.'

'Which gets us back to your birthday and the rather gorgeous Mark Jarvis.'

Allie laughed and popped the bag of waste into the bin. 'It was just a quick meal,' she lied. 'Nothing special.'

'What was nothing special?'

Her heart sank. Of all the times for him to walk in—

'Nothing.'

'Excuse me,' Anna said, and slid out, winking at Allie as she went.

'What was nothing special?' Mark said again, and Allie, sighing, turned to face him.

'Our meal last night. She was being curious—I was just saying that to get her off my back.'

He regarded her thoughtfully. 'Were you? Or did you mean it?'

She thought of lying, of covering her own emotions to protect herself, and then she looked into his eyes and knew she couldn't lie. 'No. I didn't mean it.'

'That's all right, then.' He smiled, his mouth kicking up at the corners and creasing his eyes. 'What are you doing?'

She washed her hands and scrubbed them on a paper towel. 'Just redone Darren Forsey's colostomy pouch.'

'Oh, joy. Bet you enjoyed it. I've come in to have a look at him, amongst others. How is he?'

'Fed up. He's better than he was, but he's still got to deal with the colostomy for a few weeks and endless suppositories, and I think he's going to die of embarrassment. Your little girl with appendicitis is bright and lively today, though.'

He chuckled. 'Bounced back, has she? Kids are amazing.' His smile faded as he looked at her, and he glanced down at his hands, then back to her, his eyes seeming to see right through her. 'If dinner really wasn't nothing special, how about tonight?'

She sorted out all the negatives. 'Tonight?' she repeated, her heart jiggling in her chest and a smile fighting its way onto her lips. 'What about tonight?'

'I wondered if you fancied a drink. We could grab a bar snack or something, too. There's a pub I've been told about in a village a few miles out, and it's supposed to have a really nice atmosphere. The food's supposed to be good, too.'

Should she play it cool and stall him for a week?

No. Subterfuge wasn't her thing, never had been, never would be. She let the smile escape. 'Sounds great. What time?'

'Seven again? I could pick you up, now I know where you live.'

'Anna will be unbearably curious.'

'Anna needs a lover,' he said firmly.

'Mmm. I think she fancied you for the job.'

His neck went an interesting shade of brick. 'Tough,' he murmured. 'Right, must get on. Where's Darren? In his room?'

'Yes—just opposite the nursing station, in the single room. Can you manage?'

'You keep asking me that. No faith,' he said drily, and she watched him go, stifling a sigh of sheer enjoyment. It wasn't just adolescent fantasy, he was good-looking. Very decorative. She eyed the soft, thick hair on his head. It was the colour of a gold nugget, not bright, just warm and interesting and tinged with fair bits where the sun had bleached it. It looked infinitely touchable—

And she was in danger of losing her job and her marbles if she didn't pull herself together!

She cleared away the last of her bits and pieces, washed her hands again and went out into the ward. There was a baby crying, little Amy Fulcher, who was in under observation after severe abdominal pain with no obvious cause.

Her mother had gone outside for a short walk in the fresh air, and Allie scooped up the eighteen-month-old and cuddled her, walking her up and down and crooning to her until she settled again. Poor little scamp was exhausted, because she'd been crying off and on all night. It seemed likely that the surgeon in charge of her case would decide to operate today to investigate, but the baby seemed reasonably well apart from the pain.

Mark came over to her as she was settling the baby down against her shoulder, and brushed his hand lightly over her head. 'Poor little scrap. They're going to X-ray her again,' he told her. 'Apparently they think she might have bands or adhesions around the intestines.'

'Mmm. She's a bit old for bands to suddenly be a problem at eighteen months, and she hasn't had any previous surgery to give her adhesions, but it could be, I suppose. The symptoms fit. It's obviously not that bad because she's not shocky or vomiting—'

Flying in the face of God, she thought a second later, as Amy retched and covered her uniform in green bile.

'OK, I take that back. Thank you, darling. How lovely. Shh, sweetheart, it's all right now,' Allie said under her breath, soothing the baby automatically. She went quiet, and Allie laid her down in the cot and looked at her shoulder and chest in despair. She'd deal with it later. Just now she had to wipe the baby's mouth and make sure she was all right.

Certainly the crying had stopped. Mark looked over her shoulder.

'Well, it seems to have done the trick—she's more comfortable now,' he said thoughtfully.

'Jolly good. I'm so glad one of us is.'

He chuckled, and patted her other shoulder. 'You smell gorgeous.'

'Thank you so much,' she said with a huge false smile. 'I can't tell you what it's like from this side.'

'Did someone chuck on you, Nurse?' one of the boys asked, cruising past on crutches and regarding her uniform with undisguised mirth.

'Just a bit. How's your leg?'

'Excellent. I can go home today, maybe, if the X-ray's all right.'

'Good. That's great.' It was. Healthy young boys with damaged limbs were a nightmare to entertain and keep quiet, but fortunately for the most part they healed at a huge rate of knots and thus weren't such a drastic problem.

'You just want to get rid of me,' he said mournfully, and Allie laughed.

'You guessed, Tim.'

Tim flashed her a grin and set off again. He was getting too darned good on those crutches—

'Can I make a suggestion?'

Allie glanced up at Mark, glowering at his twinkling eyes and twitching mouth.

'Change my clothes, perhaps?'

'You guessed.' He smiled. 'Great minds, eh?'

She sniffed, curled up her nose expressively and headed for the sluice.

'I'll just strip this tabard off and find a clean shirt, then I'll be back to write that lot up. I don't suppose you'd like to report it to the surgical team? Oh, and find someone to sort Amy out?'

'Sure.' Mark grinned, waggled his fingers and went into the office to use the phone, and Allie dealt with the little crisis to her person, washed her hands for the thousandth time that day and pulled on a clean shirt from the stores.

'Hi-ho,' she mumbled, tugging the clean tabard straight and heading back to the ward.

Mark sniffed and smiled. 'Better.'

'All part of the job,' she said with a grin. 'I'll go and check on Amy. I just dropped her, poor little kid. Did you find anyone to sort her out?'

'Anna's gone to do it.'

'Thanks.' She flashed him a grateful smile and went to see how Amy was now. Anna was still with her, changing her and settling her on a clean draw-sheet.

'OK?'

Allie smiled. 'Yes, thanks. I always get in the way.'

'Don't we all? Her mother's on the way back—I rang the coffee shop and asked them to tell her. She'd just nipped in for breakfast. The surgical reg is on his way down—I think they may operate this morning now.'

Allie nodded. 'I wondered. Still, she's on nil by mouth already, so there's no delay.'

Mrs Fulcher arrived back then, and Allie left Anna talking to her and went to see what else she could find. As sure as eggs, there'd be plenty.

It was after four before she got away, not the three o'clock her shift should have ended, but they'd had a flood of post-ops back from General Surgery and Orthopaedics, and she'd had to say goodbye to Tim, and what with one thing and another the time had just slipped by.

She went home and threw her washing together and walked to the laundrette round the corner, read an out-of-date magazine while the clothes sloshed round in the machine and then read another one while the tumble dryer finished the job. She didn't get home until half past six, and then had to plead with Lucy for the bathroom.

Consequently she was late—which was a nuisance because it meant Lucy got to answer the door and let Mark in, and Allie was like a cat on hot bricks while she finished getting ready, wondering what she was saying.

She needn't have worried. Lucy, predictably, was talking about herself, and Mark was looking polite. Funny how she could read him already—or did she mean still?

She flashed him a smile. 'Hi. Sorry I'm late—I had to go to the laundrette and do the dreaded washing.'

'That's OK.' He stood up and smiled at her flat-mate. 'Nice to meet you, Lucy,' he murmured, and taking Allie's arm, he ushered her out of the door.

His car was outside—a very normal, ordinary car, nothing too big, just a sensible car for the town. She was surprised. She would have expected him to have a—well, a sexier car, somehow, but what? A Ferrari, for heaven's sake? A Mercedes?

He was only an SHO.

And that was another thing that was puzzling her. Surely by now he should have been a registrar? Unless he'd taken time out for something else... She'd have to ask.

He opened the passenger door for her, went round and slid behind the wheel. Suddenly the car seemed much smaller, and astonishingly intimate.

'All set?' he asked, throwing her a grin, and she nodded.

'Where are we going?'

'Pulham St Peter. It's just north of here, and the pub's very good, so I'm told.'

Pulham wasn't far. She settled back against the actually very comfortable seat and watched him out of the corner of her eye. Within seconds she was totally relaxed. He was a good driver, quiet, competent and not hasty, but he didn't hang about, either.

She realised she felt safe, and it was a strange feeling. She was normally edgy with other people driving her. She didn't have long to worry about it, though, because they were pulling up in the pub car park in no time, and he was ushering her into the busy, crowded bar.

It was noisy and full, but by a miracle another couple vacated a table in the corner just as they had got their drinks and they were able to sit down out of the way and study the menu.

'Shall we eat in here, or in the restaurant?' he asked her.

Conscious of the price and the fact that tonight she was *definitely* going halves, she said, 'In here, I think.'

He nodded, scanned the menu again and looked at her. 'Decided yet?'

'Scampi and chips—and I'm paying for mine.'

He chuckled. 'How did I know that?'

He went to the bar armed with her money and placed the order and paid, and then came back and handed her her change. 'There you are, you stubborn, independent young woman.'

She smiled and pocketed the money. She felt better now. She didn't want to feel she owed him anything. Not that he would take advantage, but there had been the odd occasion in her past where a man had felt he had a right to her body because she'd accepted a meal from him. It hadn't taken her long to dissuade her erstwhile suitors, but it had left a nasty taste in the mouth, and she didn't want to mess up their budding relationship—

'Penny for them.'

She laughed. 'Not a chance. What are you having?'

'Same as you.'

Their eyes clashed, and she looked away, her heart hammering. Oh, Lord. It would be so easy to fall for him. She cast around for a neutral topic of conversation, and remembered her thoughts about his career progression.

'Tell me about your work,' she said, sipping her drink. 'How come you're still an SHO? I would have thought you'd be a registrar by now.'

He grinned wryly. 'I would have been, but I changed horses in the middle of the race. Well, actually, I changed races. You know I wanted to do general surgery, like my father?'

She nodded. 'Yes, I remember. You were keen.'

'I was—until I started doing it. Then I felt curiously detached from it all. The patients come in with a problem that someone else has detected, you fix it, and they go away. You never see them again, never know how they are unless there's a problem.'

'But that's good. If you don't see them again, you've done your job.'

He shook his head. 'Maybe—but it's not the job I want to be doing. I want to find the problem, send them to get it sorted and follow it up afterwards at home.'

'But that's general practice,' she said, a little bemused.

'Exactly.'

She stared at him in astonishment. 'But you're going to be a surgeon.'

He shook his head. 'No. Not any more. That's why I'm doing paeds, why I've done obs and gynae, and A&E, and general medicine, and geriatrics—'

'You want to be a GP?' she said slowly, the penny finally dropping.

He smiled. 'Yes—why not?'

Why not? She thought of the stress her father was under, of his partner who had found the strain all too much and taken the easy way out, leaving his wife and two young children to cope alone without him—

'Why not?' she said incredulously. 'Because it's an awful life, that's why not. It's dreadful. That's why they can't recruit GPs for love nor money. It's stressful, it's bogged down with paperwork, the hours are horrendous, it's a thankless task—'

'No. It's not a thankless task. It might be all the other things, but it's not a thankless task, and the hours are much better now. Nearly all GPs are in co-operatives, so their time on call is much better organised and less stressful.'

She snorted. 'Talk to my father about it.'

'I have—I did. He agrees.'

'No, he doesn't. Well, he might have done five years ago, but he doesn't now. Why do you think he's taking early retirement?'

Mark shrugged. 'To enjoy the rest of his life while he still can?'

She snorted again. 'Not my father. He's a workaholic. No, it's stress, I know it is.'

'Well, whatever, it's what I want to do, Allie,' he said quietly, straightening the edge of his beermat with a strong, blunt fingertip. 'I'm not cut out for hospital medicine, I know that now.'

She was stunned. Shocked, confused, utterly baffled by his announcement. He was going to be a surgeon. She'd always known that. It was who he was—wasn't it?

She sipped her drink again absently, and then the barmaid called out a number and Mark stood up, coming back moments later with two fragrant, steaming baskets of scampi and chips nestled on absorbent paper napkins, two wooden forks and a selection of condiments in another basket.

'Here—it smells gorgeous.'

It did. Fattening, wicked and absolutely lovely. She let her breath out on a quiet sigh, sprinkled salt liberally over her food with total disregard for her health, and tucked in.

A GP, for heaven's sake—

'Allie?'

She looked up, searching his face for any clue that he'd been winding her up, and found none.

'What?'

'What's the matter?'

Was she so easy to read? She shrugged. 'I just thought—I don't know. I always knew you were going to be a surgeon.'

He grinned. 'Well, I'm not. Believe me, I was shocked as well. You'll get over it. The scampi's good. Do you want some tartare sauce?'

'Mmm.' She tore the corner off the packet and squeezed it out mechanically, then stuck the little wooden fork into a piece of scampi and bit into it. He was right, it was good. She put thoughts of his career out of her mind and concentrated on eating and enjoying his company, but something had gone, like a light being switched off inside her.

It was only later, after he'd taken her home and given her another of those sizzling kisses on the door-step, that she realised why.

They had no future, because there was no way she could spend her life with anyone who was going into general practice. There was no way she'd marry him if things went that far. She couldn't bring children into the world knowing their father might not last the course. She'd seen at first hand the havoc it could cause in a woman's life, and she had no intention of letting it happen to her.

Then she chided herself for being ridiculous.

You're getting a bit ahead of yourself, Allie Baker. You've had two dates—and one of them didn't even really count. Stop acting like he's asked you to marry him!

She got ready for bed, climbed under the chilly duvet and snuggled down, and waited fruitlessly for sleep to come.

They had a new admission the next day, a little girl of seven from the cystic fibrosis clinic. Claudia Hall had been diagnosed with CF at birth, and was currently struggling with yet another deep-seated chest infection.

She was coming in for intravenous antibiotics to combat it, and Allie greeted her and her very pregnant mother affectionately. It was the second time she'd been in in the few months Allie had been on the ward, the last time to insert a gastrostomy tube in her stomach so she could have special feeds delivered by pump overnight to boost the amount she was able to eat, because her appetite was dreadful and she wasn't able to take in enough to sustain herself.

Everybody thought CF was just a chest condition, Allie mused, and yet it affected the intestines just as much, causing havoc with the assimilation of food and secretion of enzymes. In fact if Claudia ate anything with fat in it, she took handfuls of enzyme pills to enable her to digest it properly. Between the enzymes and the tube feeds, Claudia had been gaining weight, but now she'd lost it again with this infection. Allie had hoped they wouldn't have to see her again so soon, and it was a shame. She'd had more than enough to deal with already in her short life.

'Where am I this time?' the little girl asked as she looked round the all too familiar ward.

'Nice bed by the window—that do you?' Allie said with a smile.

Claudia nodded. 'Yes, please. I don't want to be in the Winnie the Pooh room again.'

Allie laughed. 'Well, you won't have to this time because you're MRSA free, so we won't have to isolate you. How's Piglet?'

Claudia pulled up her jumper and showed Allie her gastrostomy tube, nicknamed Piglet because of the Winnie the Pooh room she'd been put in when she'd gone down with the MRSA infection in the gastrostomy site. 'He's fine. Still eating all night.'

'Good. Right, we need to admit you and do all the paperwork, then you can go and find out who's in the playroom.'

'Is Katie still here?' she asked.

Allie shook her head. 'No, sorry. She went home a few weeks ago. There are a couple of girls of your age, though. I'm sure you'll get on with them.'

Claudia nodded and scrambled up onto the bed, triggering a coughing fit that ended in her vomiting. Allie was prepared. It was a frequent occurrence with CF children, and she was ready with a paper bowl.

'She's really gone downhill the last few days,' her mother Jayne explained. 'She's been coughing more and more—Dr Barrett thought she should come in and get it sorted. She's got pneumonia this time—I suppose it makes a change from pseudomonas.'

Allie nodded. 'Yes, she's down for gentamycin. That should clobber it. Can't have you feeling this poorly, can we?' she said with a smile for Claudia, who was flopped against the backrest looking exhausted.

'She hasn't been sleeping all that much,' Jayne said, and Allie could tell by the bags under her eyes that Jayne hadn't, either.

'When's the new baby due?' she asked.

'Three weeks, but I may not make it that long. I've got dodgy ligaments in my pelvis and it's so painful. I have to wear a belt round my hips to support it, and it's getting really tiresome, not to mention difficult to move around, so they might induce me early.'

As if the poor woman didn't have enough on her plate. 'It'll soon be over,' Allie said comfortingly, and then turned back to Claudia. 'All right, poppet? Feeling a bit better?'

She nodded, but it was only politeness. She looked awful, poor kid, and Allie wanted to hug her.

'Dr Jarvis'll be here in a minute, I expect, and he'll check you over and get your IV line in. Then we can get some bug-zapper into you and you should start to feel a bit better.'

Claudia nodded again, and Allie flipped open her

file and took out the sheet at the front with all the labels on. They were printed with name, address, next of kin, hospital number and so forth, and were stuck on anything to do with the patient. It saved hours of copying and potential inaccuracy—when they were right.

Allie checked, on the principle that one could never be too sure. 'Are all your details still the same? Address, phone number and so on?'

Jayne nodded. 'Yes, nothing's changed.'

'Good.' She stuck Claudia's labels on the charts, clipped them to the end of the bed and took her temperature and blood pressure. The respirations she'd already done surreptitiously while Jayne had been talking, and they were up, as she'd expected.

'Fancy a cup of tea?' she asked Jayne when she'd finished.

'Oh, I'd love one. Can I make it?'

Allie shook her head. 'You sit there, I'll find someone to do it for you. Weak, black, no sugar—is that right?'

'How did you remember that?' Jayne asked softly, and looked near to tears. Allie guessed that this pregnancy had been very difficult for her. She had a horrendous obstetric history, by all accounts, and it was touch and go whether this one would be all right. Still, at least she was almost there. That was a huge improvement.

'I have a very retentive memory for useless information,' she told Jayne now, and with a smile, she left them alone and found Pearl, the Jamaican ward orderly. 'You couldn't take a cuppa to Jayne Hall, could you? She's over there. Weak, black, no sugar.'

'I remember, darlin', don't worry. I know Jayne

very well. Sometimes I think she lives here. Sure, I'll take her a cup of tea. I was just goin' to ask her myself.'

Allie left Jayne in Pearl's capable hands, and thought not for the first time what a gift to the ward the matronly woman was. She was possessed of infinite kindness and patience, and seemed to be able to keep order with the bored and naughty children absolutely effortlessly. They all adored her, and it was mutual. She would have made a wonderful nurse, but perhaps she was more useful as an orderly, because she never had to do anything unpleasant to the children and that made her easier to trust.

Allie checked on Amy Fulcher who had come back from Theatre yesterday after she'd gone off duty. She was looking better already, much more comfortable, and her mother was slumped in the big vinyl armchair beside her, sleeping.

It seemed a shame to wake either of them, so Allie left them to it for a little while. Sleep was probably more useful than anything to the baby at the moment, and the mother was exhausted.

She looked across at Claudia's bed and saw Mark had arrived and was chatting to them. He had one hip hitched up on the edge of the bed, and he was smiling and teasing Claudia into smiling back. He was good with children, she realised, and wondered why he didn't go into paediatric surgery.

He'd been so keen, so certain of his choice—

She shook her head. She was still stunned by his revelation, and was trying to reconcile herself to the bitter fact that there could be no future for them beyond the immediate one of a few dates—except maybe, because he was the only man she'd ever felt like this about, a brief affair.

Nothing lasting. Nothing permanent. No happy ever after. Just something to remember him by when he moved on.

She swallowed hard and found herself something to do at the other end of the ward, away from him and his laughing eyes and wide, ready smile that made the sun come out.

Her reprieve was short-lived, though, because he asked her to assist him with Claudia's intravenous line. He was putting in a long line, not as long as a Hickman line that went all the way to the heart, but one that went into the arm in the crook of the elbow and up into the top of the chest.

'As you know it lasts longer than a needle cannula,' he explained to Jayne and Claudia, 'and this treatment's going to take a couple of weeks. We don't want to have to keep putting in another line and messing you about, do we, Claudia?'

Claudia shook her head, and they moved her into the treatment room where they undertook the more sterile procedures. Allie was the 'clean' nurse, and a younger staff nurse was the 'dirty' nurse, the one who handled the outside of the packets and opened them for Allie, who was scrubbed and gowned and ready to assist.

Mark scrubbed as well, and then they settled down with Claudia to insert the line into her little arm. It was splinted straight, and would stay like that until the line came out, which was a bit restricting but one of the penalties for not having to have the line changed constantly.

Her mother was there, of course, supportive as

ever, and Allie wondered how Mark would deal with Claudia and her independent attitude. Her mother had brought her up as far as possible with input and control over her illness, and her quiet courage and calm dignity were terrifying.

As for Mark, it was the first time Allie had seen him doing any procedure, and she was impressed. Claudia cried, of course, but only a little, and he was very kind and gentle with her, and it was over in no time. Allie secured the end of the line with tape and made sure the splint that kept her elbow straight was comfortable, and then she was given the first dose of antibiotic through it.

It seemed such a shame to have to put her through it, Allie thought sadly, but it was a small price to pay to combat the germs in her chest which were playing havoc with her breathing and damaging the already fragile structure of her lungs.

'All right now?' Mark asked, checking his handiwork and smiling at Claudia.

She nodded, looking wan and exhausted against the white pillows. Allie wanted to cry for her. She wanted to cry for all of them, but she couldn't, of course, so she smiled and hugged and dished out sensible advice and struggled on.

Just like Jayne, she thought with sympathy, struggling on with her softened pelvic ligaments so that every movement made the two ends of her pubic bones scrape together at the synthesis, the join in the middle at the front. It wasn't a joint anyone was ever aware of, unless something like this happened.

It must be horribly painful and difficult, Allie thought with another surge of sympathy as she pushed the bed back to its place in the ward. Still, not for much longer. It would soon recover once the pregnancy hormones disappeared from her system.

'Can I go and see who's in the playroom?' Claudia asked her, and Allie nodded.

'If you want to. Take a paper hat with you, just in case you're sick. Want me to introduce you to the others?'

She shook her head. '"S OK,' she said pragmatically. 'I'll do it.'

'She's so independent,' Jayne said in admiration, sinking into the big armchair by the bed. 'You'd think she'd be clingy, but she's not. She just gets on with it, no matter how awful. She's got such guts—'

Jayne broke off, her lips pressed together in a firm line, and Allie wondered what it must be like to have a child with CF and know there was a one-in-four chance that the baby she carried would have inherited the same dreadful and debilitating disease.

She patted her shoulder, giving quiet comfort and support, and then left her to grab a few precious moments alone to rest in the comfy chair. Allie reckoned she'd earned it.

She managed to slip up to the canteen for lunch, by a miracle, and was sitting propped up in an easy chair in the corner nursing a cup of tea when Beth strolled over.

'He's gorgeous,' she said without preamble. 'I saw him today in Outpatients. I had to cover. He is just luscious.'

Allie didn't pretend not to understand. 'I know,' she said glumly.

Beth dropped into the chair opposite and gave her a curious look. 'What's the matter?' she asked. 'I'm the one that should have the long face. At least he's

interested in you—he wouldn't have noticed if I'd got
six legs!'

Allie laughed. 'Beth, you're silly. He's going to be
a GP,' she added after a pause.

'How wonderful. There are far too few of them out
there.'

'I don't want him to be a GP. It's so stressful.'

'Isn't that rather for him to decide?' Beth said
pointedly. 'And anyway, what does it matter? He's
here now, he's giving out all the right messages—
you'd have to be mad to ignore it. Well, mad or dead
or totally sexless.'

Beth was right—and Allie wasn't any of those
things, at least not where Mark was concerned.
Well—mad, maybe, but that was different.

She finished her tepid tea and set the cup down.
Happy ever after was probably a figment of the imagination, anyway, but there was no time like the present. Who said every relationship worth having had to
end in marriage?

She gave the bemused Beth a dazzling smile.
'You're a love. See you later.'

And feeling much brighter than she had all day,
she went back to work.

CHAPTER THREE

HE DIDN'T ask her out again until the weekend, and she was beginning to wonder if her imagination had read more into their relationship than was warranted.

If you could call it a relationship.

Maybe she'd presumed too much from their slight acquaintance. Maybe Anna was more appealing to him than he'd let on—although there was no sign of anything blossoming there either, she thought, and told herself that the only reason Mark had shown so much interest in her was because he was lonely in Audley and didn't know anyone else!

So she put it out of her mind, and carried on with her work and tried not to notice when he was around, but it was pointless. Her radar wouldn't switch off, and she was constantly aware of every breath he took when he was on the ward.

Still, her patients were a good distraction, and she tried to concentrate on them.

Little Claudia Hall was doing all right on her antibiotics, despite feeling sick, and her mother and father had taken over her antibiotic therapy and were giving her the injections through the catheter in her arm. It saved the nursing staff a job, and her parents were already so involved with their daughter's care that they were utterly reliable.

In any case they were probably more knowledge-able about her condition than many of the staff on the ward, and like so many parents these days, wanted to know everything and not be kept in the dark. Furthermore they explained everything to Claudia, so that she could be in control of her treatment.

As Jayne said, 'She's Claudia first, and CF second. All this treatment isn't for the CF, it's for Claudia. She has to understand it and condone it and accept it. It's her body, not yours, not mine. She has to make the choices, and if she's given some control, it helps her to deal with it.'

However their philosophy could only help so much. One of the hardest things was also one of the simplest, in comparison to the other things she had to endure. Every third day of her gentamycin therapy, she had to have pre- and post-gentamycin blood tests to make sure that her fragile little system was able to cope with the drug.

The blood was taken from one of her hands, from the one she herself had chosen having examined them and seen which looked best. She would then rub in 'magic cream', a local anaesthetic cream that would numb the area a little so the needle didn't hurt so much.

It was a tough regime, and after all the other things she had to put up with, it was odd that it was the plasters that upset her more than anything. She didn't like the needles, but most particularly she didn't like having the plasters taken off, and they had to be removed on her count of three.

Claudia's count. Nobody else's. Tough, gutsy little kid that she was, she was definitely in control, and her sense of humour and courage were legendary on the ward.

Jayne's courage was pretty awe-inspiring, as well. Her pelvis was making it very difficult for her to get around, and Allie felt sorry for her. As if being that pregnant and having another child sick in hospital wasn't enough, she thought, without having anything else to cope with.

Darren Forsey had recovered well physically from his operation, and his abscess was much more comfortable now, but he was quiet and withdrawn and wouldn't go out amongst the others because of the colostomy bag. It didn't seem to matter how many times Allie told him it didn't smell or show under his dressing gown, he was still horribly conscious of it.

Oddly enough it was Mark who talked him round and persuaded him out of his room in the end. He told him about a children's television announcer who'd had it done, and a singer, both people he'd heard of.

'They wouldn't get very far if they wouldn't go out, would they?' he pointed out reasonably, and Darren spent a while thinking about this, then told Allie out of the blue on Friday morning that he wanted to go into the playroom and see if there was anything interesting on TV.

'They've got satellite TV in there,' he explained, when Allie asked as casually as possibly what was wrong with his own set.

And that was that. She waited while he wrapped himself up in his dressing gown, carefully disguising the little bulge of the bag, and walked down to the playroom with him. The teacher had just finished for the morning, and the children in there were lively and hardly noticed Darren.

'That's Peter over there with the red hair, and the boy with the sling on is Adrian, and that girl is Claudia. Want me to stay and introduce you?'

He shook his head, and she left him to it, sensing that he wanted to blend into the background at first. He'd introduce himself when he was ready, and if it all got too much he could find his own way back to bed.

She went out of the door looking over her shoulder at him and bumped—literally—into Mark.

His hands came up to steady her, and he smiled that gorgeous smile and made her heart flip-flop. 'I was just looking for you,' he told her.

'I'm here,' she said, a little breathless and cross with herself because of it. He'd shown quite clearly all week that he wasn't interested.

'Are you busy tonight?'

She blinked. 'Tonight? No, I don't think so.' She knew quite well she wasn't, but it didn't hurt to be a little vague. 'Why?'

He grinned. 'I just thought it was time to come up for air. I've been working and studying for the last two nights, and I think I need a night off. I wondered if you wanted to join me.'

'Where? For what?' she asked, pretending that she was considering it.

'Whatever,' he said with a little shrug. 'I'll leave it up to you. A meal, dancing, cinema, clubbing, quiet pub, evening in watching telly—anything but reading medical textbooks, really!'

'Well, that broadens the field,' she said with a chuckle. 'Yeah, sounds fine. I'll think about what we could do—my housemates might have an idea. I'll see Beth at lunchtime probably. She's quite good at finding interesting things to do in this town. She gets more practice than I do.'

'Poor baby,' he teased, his eyes twinkling, and she could have kicked herself for being so honest.

'Some of us go to bed at night,' she said primly, and the twinkle grew brighter.

'Sounds better and better,' he murmured, and she felt a wave of soft colour working its way up her throat and spreading relentlessly across her face.

'You know what I mean,' she said even more primly, and he chuckled.

'Unfortunately yes. It's the story of my life. I tell you what, if you don't see me before then, come and find me in my room when you've decided what we're doing, and I'll dress accordingly. I'm in room eighteen—I should be there from about five-thirty. Is that OK?'

She nodded. 'Sure. I'll do that.'

And maybe, in his room, she'd find a few clues to his personality, to the man he was now. Even if they were only going to indulge in a brief liaison, she wanted more foundation to it than just a rush of hormones.

After all, even colleagues needed to be able to talk to each other!

'Come in!'

She opened the door, and found Mark dressed only in a pair of jeans, bare feet sticking out of the bottom, a towel slung round his neck. 'Hi,' he said with a grin. 'You've caught me—I'm just this second out of the shower. So what are we doing?'

She shrugged, distracted by the glimpse of firm, muscled chest through the gap between the ends of the towel. His body was still beaded with moisture, and as she watched a tiny dribble picked its way carefully down his chest, zigzagging through the fine scatter of hair to melt into the waistband of his jeans.

She dragged her eyes up to his and coloured softly. 'Um—I don't know. Beth wasn't around, and I didn't see Lucy either, so I didn't get to ask their advice.'

He propped his bottom on the edge of the windowsill and crossed his ankles, hands wrapped round the ends of the towel, a natural, relaxed, sexy pose that shot her blood pressure up into the gods.

'So what do you fancy?' he asked, and she gulped. Down, girl, she told herself. He doesn't mean that!

She shrugged. 'Um—whatever,' she said, and then found her mouth running away with her unbiddden. 'Beth and Lucy will be out tonight at a party—you could come to my house and I could cook for you,' she suggested.

A smile lit his eyes. 'Home-cooked food—what a luxury. That sounds lovely. Are you sure?'

She must be insane! 'Yes, that's fine,' she said, as casually as she could manage, and wondered what on earth she was going to give him. The larder was empty—it was always empty! She'd have to whip round to the supermarket and find something that didn't take hours of preparation.

'Anything in particular you want to eat?' she asked with false calm, and prayed that he'd say something she could cook. The kitchen wasn't her strong point—

'Anything. Whatever you fancy. I'm not fussy— just not liver, kidneys or baked beans. Anything else.'

She nodded, and backed towards the door. 'Seventhirty?' she suggested, trying to keep her eyes off the wall of muscle advancing towards her.

He took the edge of the door in his hand and smiled. He was just inches away, and she could see the pulse beating in his throat. A dribble of water ran across it, and she had to physically stop herself from licking it away.

'Fine. I'll look forward to it,' he said, and bending slightly, he brushed her lips with his.

Heat shot through her, and with a fleeting smile, she turned and all but ran down the corridor. All that sex appeal coming for supper, and she was going to be locked up alone with him.

She might not survive it!

Mark rang the doorbell again, hefted the bottle of wine in his hand and wondered what was keeping her. He heard footsteps behind him, someone running down the street, and he turned just as she reached the end of the front path, a small brown paper bag in her hand.

She smiled distractedly up at him and rummaged for her keys. 'Hi—sorry. Have you been here long? I forgot cream for the sauce. Come in.'

She was breathless and windblown, her cheeks flushed with the cold and running, her eyes sparkling, and she looked lovely. God give me the strength to keep my hands to myself, he thought, and shifted his gaze from the wild rise and fall of her breasts under the soft fleece.

There were enticing smells coming from the kitchen, and he followed her down the hall and into the little and somewhat primitive room at the back of the house. It was freshly painted, but it was no designer kitchen, that was for sure, he thought. Still, it was clean as an operating theatre and as homely as they could make it, and the food smelt divine.

'Can I help?' he asked, plonking the bottle of wine down in the middle of the table.

'Oh—yes please. You could lay the table—oh, wine! Thanks, I'd forgotten, but you needn't have bothered—'

'Why not? You have,' he pointed out fairly, waving at the cooker, and she smiled and softened and stopped being brisk. It made her even more lovely.

'Thank you,' she murmured, and her voice was husky and scraped over his nerve-endings like fine sandpaper. Lord, she was gorgeous. He felt his jeans beginning to feel the strain of his enthusiasm, and shifted, clearing his throat.

'Where's the cutlery?'

'In here.' She pulled open a drawer right beside her, and he went and stood within inches of her and through the mouthwatering aroma of some delicious-looking concoction, he caught the faintest hint of fragrance. Soap? Perfume? Skin?

He almost groaned aloud, and grabbing cutlery he headed for the safety of the table, retreating behind it and sitting down before he embarrassed them both. She handed him a corkscrew and two glasses, and while she poked and prodded at the stove, he opened the wine, a nicely chilled Chardonnay, and filled the glasses, sliding one across the table towards her.

'Here. Have a sip.'

She smiled gratefully, took a glug and smiled again. 'Oh, it's lovely. Thank you. I'd forgotten to buy any.'

'My pleasure,' he murmured, and raised his glass. 'To reunions—and us,' he said softly, and if he hadn't known better, he would have sworn she blushed.

*   *   *

He really was so easy to be with, she thought with an inward sigh of relief as they reached the end of their meal without mishap. She'd burned nothing, ruined nothing, and he seemed to have enjoyed it.

Wonders would never cease.

She stacked the plates into the sink, put the coffee on and, to stop him from washing up, she steered him out of the kitchen and into the sitting room, pushing him down onto the sofa. He grabbed her wrist on the way down and tugged, so that she ended up laughing beside him, wedged against his solid warmth, and before she knew what was happening his mouth brushed hers and he smiled.

'That was a wonderful meal. Thanks.'

Her heart slammed against her ribs and she gave him a distracted smile. How many megawatts did that kiss pack? And it was only a quick peck, for heaven's sake!

'My pleasure.' She shifted round so she was curled in the other corner of the sofa, her feet tucked under her, feeling a little safer with some distance between them.

'I get a feeling of *déjà vu*,' she told him. 'Five years ago we spent hours like this, putting the world to rights.'

'I know. We didn't do a very good job, did we?'

His smile was tip-tilted and sexy, and her breath stopped in her throat. She gave a strangled little laugh. 'I was awful, I kept you up for hours,' she said softly, looking down at her hands. 'I didn't give you any peace.'

'You were lovely. You are lovely. And I enjoyed our conversations.'

She laughed again, remembering his gentle under-

standing. 'You were very patient, and you were a cap-
tive audience. I thought you were wonderful,' she
confessed quietly.

'Was that why you came on to me?'

'Oh, Lord, was it so obvious?' She blushed. 'I
didn't even know I was doing it, really, I was so
naïve. I'm sorry.'

'Don't apologise. Do you have any idea how much
I wanted to take you up on your invitation?'

She felt the colour rising again, and squirmed in
the corner. 'I didn't even know what I was inviting,'
she confessed. 'Not really. I think if you hadn't been
such a gentleman about it, I would have died of
fright.'

He chuckled. 'I don't think I slept the entire fort-
night. I kept imagining what was under that very de-
mure dressing gown, and it played hell with my
sleep—and my conscience.'

'I had no idea,' she said ruefully, shaking her head.
'Even when you kissed me goodbye when you left
us, I thought you were just humouring me.'

He gave a strangled laugh. 'Humouring you?
Hardly. I just had to kiss you goodbye, and it didn't
do me a scrap of good. It just tortured my imagination
for years, and when I did finally kiss you properly,
the other day—well, what can I say? Even my vivid
imagination didn't do it justice.'

Heat sizzled between them, and Allie couldn't
breathe. She felt her heart thrashing against her ribs,
her eyes were locked with his, and when he reached
out to her, she was helpless.

She lifted her hand, felt his fingers lock onto hers
and pull her gently towards him, and she half slid,
half fell across his lap so that her hair was draped

over his arm and she was on her back, looking up into those wonderful grey eyes like pebbles in the bottom of a mountain stream, flecked with granite and dancing with light.

'Oh, Allie,' he murmured, and his mouth came down and settled over hers, just gently, teasingly. There was nothing hurried about this kiss, nothing hasty, nothing to alarm or warn her. It was just a tender, slow meeting of lips, a hesitant dance, with just the merest suggestion of passion simmering in the background.

'You taste wonderful,' he murmured, lifting his head after a moment. 'Mind if I join you down there?'

She shook her head, and he eased out from under her shoulders and stood up, kicked off his shoes and lay down beside her, drawing her back into his arms with a heartfelt sigh. 'Bliss,' he said softly, and his mouth found hers again, sipping and teasing, tormenting her until she was shaking with a desire she'd never even dreamt of.

One strong, heavy thigh eased between hers, and he rocked against her, a deep groan rumbling from his chest. She nearly cried out, arching against him and clinging to his shoulders as sensation washed over her. He felt so good against her, so big and strong and solid and right.

He lifted his head, staring down at her as he brushed her hair away from her brow with gentle fingers. His mouth was soft and bruised looking, the expression in his eyes naked and open, vulnerable. 'So lovely,' he murmured, and kissed her again.

Nothing, but nothing, could have prepared her for the onslaught of that kiss. It turned her bones to mush, scrambled her brain and made rash promises that her body believed utterly. She was helpless in his arms. She would have done anything he asked of her.

She would have stepped out of a plane for him at thirty thousand feet without a parachute, if he'd asked her to.

He asked for nothing, just kissed her until her brain was putty, then tucked her head under his chin so she could hear the pounding of his heart and held her there, cradled against his chest, until their breathing steadied and the passion in them cooled to a steady simmer.

'About an hour ago, were you making coffee?' he asked softly.

Coffee? she thought. He can think about coffee? 'Mmm. It will have been ready for ages.'

'I'll get it.'

He kissed her again, just a brief peck, and stood up and left her there, boneless and curiously peaceful despite the frustration that stalked her body like a wild cat. He was gone a few minutes, and came back with a tray holding coffee and a packet of wafer-thin mints.

'Where did they come from?' she asked, sitting up and swinging her legs over the edge of the sofa, suddenly alert.

'My coat pocket.'

'They're my favourite,' she said, half accusingly.

'I know.' He was positively smug. 'You ate thousands at the bistro on Monday.'

She laughed. 'You remembered.'

'I remember everything about you,' he said, tearing the packet open, and although it was said in a light-hearted way, she sensed that he meant it. It made her feel special. She wriggled to the edge of the sofa and

took her coffee from him, dunking the slivers of chocolate in it and sucking them.

'That's disgusting,' he said fondly. 'You always
dunked everything.'

'Mmm. Try it—they taste best like that.'

'No way. I like them cold and crisp and crunchy.'

He sat beside her, slinging his arm loosely round
her waist and hugging her. She leant back against
him, absorbing the warmth of his body and thinking
how wonderful it was to feel so relaxed with him, and
for long moments they didn't speak, just crunched or
dunked and sipped.

Then finally, when the mints were finished and the
coffee was cold, he drained his mug and put it down.

'More?' she offered, but he shook his head.

'No. I'm bushed, I need an early night. What are
you doing tomorrow?'

'Tomorrow?' she said stupidly, trying to get her
brain to work against the competition from her cla-
mouring body. 'Nothing, I don't think. I'm not working—not till Sunday. Why?'

'I'm going house-hunting. I've got two cottages to
look at in Pulham. I wondered if you wanted to
come.'

She shot him a puzzled glance. 'House-hunting?'
she repeated. 'Already? How have you had time to
look?'

'Well, I haven't, much, but I'm doing my GP
trainee year in a practice just north of Pulham, about
ten miles from here, and there just happen to be a
couple of cottages up for sale. I thought it made sense
to buy, if I'm going to be in the area at least eighteen
months. I thought you might want to come and have

a laugh. I've never bought a house before. I don't really know what to look for.'

'Cracks,' she said with a smile, thinking that he was going to be in the area and she'd be able to see him. Strange the leap of joy she felt at that fact, considering how busy she was telling herself they had no future! 'Yes, I'll come,' she agreed without hesitating. 'I'd love to. I love houses. I'm not much help, but I'd love to come along just to be beaky.'

'Good. I'll pick you up at ten—the first appointment's at ten-thirty. Wear something you can walk in—I want to check out the footpaths and things if we've got time.'

'I'll bring wellies,' she promised.

He stood up and pulled her to her feet, wrapping her in his arms and kissing her soundly again, stirring up the wild cat just when it was settling down to a steady purr. Then he eased away, tweaked her nose gently and let himself out, leaving her feeling frustrated and yet satisfied at the same time.

It had been a wonderful evening, she thought as she gathered up their mugs and the empty packet from the mints. She carried them through to the kitchen and found he'd washed up when he'd come out to get the coffee.

His thoughtfulness added to the warm glow inside her, and she went up to bed and refused to think about the fact that they didn't have a future. There was plenty of time to worry about that later. For now she was just going to enjoy the present, and, as he'd suggested, see where things went.

And tomorrow, she'd see him again.

She went to sleep with the smile still on her lips.

*   *   *

The first cottage was awful. It was terraced, like the house Allie rented with her friends, but there the similarities ended. The kitchen was tiny and badly designed even though it had been recently refitted, the bedrooms were minute and gloomy, the garden was hardly big enough for the dustbin and a garden chair, and there was nowhere to park. The whole thing had been done up in someone else's taste, and she could tell by Mark's non-committal words that it wasn't his.

That was good. It wasn't hers, either. However it didn't alter the fact that the place being in good order must add significantly to the cost, even if it would have to be gutted to replace the replacement windows and doors and put back some original features. The chimneys were gone, the character had been stripped right out of it and it could have been a bad modern house.

Mark was depressed. 'The owner must be a total Philistine. I hope the other one's better,' he muttered as they walked back to the car parked miles away down the village street.

'I expect so,' she said doubtfully. 'Is it the same price?'

'No, it's more, but not enough more to make that much difference.'

He was disheartened, she could tell. It was his first house, he had a mortgage agreed in principle, he'd told her, and yet at the moment property was going so fast in his price range that anything available was gone before it was properly on the market.

'How long's this one been on?' she asked.

'The one we've just seen? A couple of months. The next one isn't on yet.'

'So that might be good news. This one must be

overpriced if it's still hanging around. Perhaps the other one will be more realistic. What's it called?'

'Church Cottage. It's down Church Lane, oddly enough. Should be easy to find.'

'Maybe it's a good omen. Perhaps God will be on your side,' she said with a reassuring smile.

'Hmm.'

He didn't sound convinced. However, when they found the next cottage down a quiet little lane, set back from the road by a tangled front garden that must once have been beautiful, Allie was entranced.

'Oh, Mark, look at it, it's lovely!' she breathed.

'It is, isn't it? I can't believe it.'

They stood for a moment, studying the soft, mellow red bricks, the original, rather tired windowframes in need of rather more than a lick of paint, the slightly crooked front door with the rose scrambling over the porch roof and bravely sporting a soft pink bloom even now, in October, and then the door opened and an elderly lady came out.

Her hair was caught back in a bun, her cardigan was buttoned up to the chin and she looked like the archetypal village postmistress.

'Dr Jarvis?' she said in a surprisingly firm voice.

'That's right,' Mark said, lifting the sticking little gate and going towards her, hand outstretched and smiling a greeting. 'You must be Mrs Pettitt.'

'Indeed I am. Come on in so we don't let the heat out. I can't bear the cold these days and the sun doesn't seem so warm any more.'

They followed her in and shut the door, and Mark introduced Allie as 'a friend and colleague'. She wasn't sure if she was disappointed by that or relieved. It was irrelevant, though. She made herself look around, and fell instantly in love.

'Oh, it's gorgeous,' she said softly.

'Isn't it?' Mark echoed, gazing around with a slightly bemused look on his face. 'What a difference. It really is delightful.'

'Well, I don't know about delightful,' Mrs Pettitt said, flushing with pride. 'I've looked after it as well as I can, which for the last few years since Harold died hasn't been very well, but it's too much for me now. I can't get upstairs any longer, so I've been sleeping down here—the bathroom's next to the kitchen, so it's all very handy for me. Go on up and have a look—there's only the two bedrooms and one's very small, so it's no good for a large family.'

'Not a problem. I don't have a family yet,' Mark assured her.

Allie followed Mark up the stairs, watching as he ducked under the beam and wondering how on earth one would get furniture up the narrow little staircase. Plank by plank, probably!

He'd come to a halt in the doorway of the bigger bedroom, craning his neck at the beams that spanned the vaulted ceiling. Cobwebs hung from the tie-beams and criss-crossed the windows, but it didn't matter. Underneath the layer of neglect it was charming, and he was in love.

'Oh, it's gorgeous, Allie,' he said, turning to her with a smile. His eyes were shining with excitement, and he looked like a kid on Christmas morning. 'I can't believe it. It's so different to the other one.'

'Yes—it's got one and a half bedrooms instead of three, the bathroom's downstairs—'

'It's detached instead of terraced, it's got parking,

room for a garage, room to extend if you wanted to—
and it's wonderful. I love it.'

'You haven't seen the kitchen yet,' she cautioned,
but he was beyond hope. He went downstairs, took a
cursory glance round the kitchen and bathroom which
were old-fashioned but functional, stuck his head out
of the back door and went back to Mrs Pettitt and
told her he wanted to buy it.

'You aren't going to haggle on the price, are you?'
she said worriedly. 'Only I'm buying a sheltered flat
with a warden, and it's quite pricey. I don't want to
be short.'

'I had no intention of haggling on the price,' he
assured her.

Mrs Pettitt smiled. 'What a relief. Still, before we
all get carried away, there is one more thing—it may
put you off, of course, but I hope not because I want
you to have the house. I think you're a kind person—
you've got kind eyes, and so has your young lady.
That's very important, because I've been here nearly
sixty years, since I first married Harold, and I have
to sell to someone I like. But, you see, it's the cat.'

Mark blinked. 'The cat?'

'I can't take her with me, there are no pets allowed.
She's got to find a new home, and she's old, like me,
and wouldn't take kindly to being messed around. So
I told my son that I'd only sell the house if I liked
the people and if they'd have Minnie. Minnie?
Minnie-Minnie-Minnie-Minnie?'

There was a clattering noise from the cat flap in
the back door, and a large black and white cat with
a condescending look on her face waddled into the
room, sat down and eyeballed them malevolently.

'This is Minnie,' Mrs Pettitt said unnecessarily.
'Minnie, say hello to Dr Jarvis and Miss Baker.'

Mark crouched down and reached out a hand, and
after a long pause for consideration Minnie got to her
feet and waddled over, sniffed him and then rubbed
herself against his hand.

'Oh, she likes you,' Mrs Pettitt said delightedly.
'She spits and bites if she doesn't.'

'Surely not,' Mark murmured, scratching the cat
behind her ears so that her eyes glazed and she purred
and dribbled ecstatically.

'Oh, yes. And she's a wonderful ratter. We haven't
had a single rat in the house since we've had her, and
we had them before once or twice. It's because of the
river, you know. We're quite close to it here—too
high to flood, but near enough for the rats to come
and raid the bins. No, you'd need a cat anyway.'

Minnie, bored with Mark, wandered over to her
mistress and was scooped up into loving arms. 'I
don't know what I'll do without her,' Mrs Pettitt said,
her eyes filling. 'Still, my son says I have to go into
a flat, and he's right. I keep having falls and I'm more
and more lonely and I've started doing silly things,
and he's worried about me. I'm not worried, if I fall
I fall, but he frets, you see.'

Allie nodded. 'I can understand he'd be concerned
about you lying on the floor with no one to find you.
Is the flat local?'

She nodded. 'Yes. It's a lovely place, I suppose,
and I've met several of the residents. They play
bridge one afternoon a week, and I'll enjoy that.
Harold and I always used to play bridge. So, what do
you think?' she asked Mark. 'Can you take on the cat
as well as the house?'

He smiled. 'If she'll tolerate me, I'm sure I can tolerate her. You'll have to tell me which vet you use and so on, and what you feed her, but I'm sure I can take her on. I'd love a cat. We always had cats at home and I miss them—even the ones that hiss and spit.'

Mrs Pettitt sighed with relief. 'Well, then, I suppose I'd better ring my son, hadn't I? I don't know what the form is, but there's someone else supposed to be coming this afternoon, and I don't want them to have it, not now I've met you.'

Mark hesitated. 'You do realise I'll have to have a survey done for the building society?' he told her. 'Although my mortgage is arranged, the house still has to be one they'd lend money on.'

'That's all right, dear,' she assured him. 'My son's a surveyor. He would have told me if there was anything wrong, and it was rewired two years ago because he was worried, and the roof's been done. I'm sure it'll be fine. I'll ring his office and cancel the other viewers, if you're sure you want it? He's the agent, you see.'

He smiled again. 'I'm sure. I've never been more sure of anything in my life.'

Mrs Pettitt heaved a sigh of relief, blinked back a tear or two and then drew herself up. 'Right. I'll phone Gerald, and then I think I've got a drop of sherry somewhere—we can drink to it.'

So she phoned her son, and Mark spoke to him, too, to find out what he should do next, and then Mrs Pettitt found a bottle of rather fine sherry and took three crystal glasses out of the cabinet and they sealed the deal.

And Allie, watching Mark simmering with excite-

ment, found herself wondering how much time she'd
spend here with him, if any, and wishing wistfully
that he wasn't going into general practice and that
they had a future together—a future here, in this
lovely cottage, surrounded by the beautiful Suffolk
countryside, the air ringing with the laughter of their
children—

Pipedreams, she told herself crossly, and forced
herself to listen to Mark and Mrs Pettitt talking about
moving dates and suchlike, and stop torturing herself
with things that would never be.

CHAPTER FOUR

MARK'S transparent happiness was infectious, and he and Allie spent the rest of the day celebrating. He insisted on taking her out for lunch—to the pub in Pulham, of course—and Allie had a feeling he'd spend a great many of his evenings in there in the future, to save having to cook.

Not that she could blame him if he did. The atmosphere was congenial, the landlord was friendly, and the locals welcomed Mark with open arms. 'Nice to have a bit of new blood in the village—but mind out for the panto crew or they'll have you conscripted before you know what's hit you,' one farmer advised with a chuckle.

'Panto?' he asked, his antennae going up, and Allie watched in amazement as he all but talked himself into it.

'I could prance about in the chorus,' he said thoughtfully, and before he knew what was what, a man in the corner was being called over and introduced to him.

'My wife's the producer. You're a fool, but if you're interested, mosey on up to Rookery Farm at eight next Wednesday—they're doing the first auditions. They're always short of men—especially young men. They have boys and they get the old fools that have run out of excuses, but young blood's always thin on the ground. I don't suppose your young lady—'

'Oh, no.' Allie shook her head vehemently. 'I'm a nurse—I work odd hours. I couldn't make the rehearsals regularly, or the performances. Sorry.' She gave what she was sure was a weak and feeble smile, and let Mark talk himself further into the mess.

Still, he seemed happy, she thought, and after all it was part of his job to integrate with the community, if he was going to be a GP. Her father had always been involved in things in the village, and her mother. It was expected, really, although she couldn't remember them ever getting involved in a pantomime. They didn't have one in their village, of course. That might have been a minor drawback!

They left the pub in mid-afternoon, drove past the delightful little cottage again and meandered along the lanes back to Audley. 'Fancy a cup of tea?' he suggested as they arrived back at the hospital. 'I've got chocolate biscuits.'

And she could get a close look at his room. She hadn't noticed it last time—too many distractions in the form of his naked chest!

'That would be lovely,' she agreed. They parked in the staff car park at the back of the hospital, and went along to his room.

'We never did go for a walk,' he said with a smile as he let her in. 'How about tomorrow?'

She wrinkled her nose. 'I'm working from seven till three. It'll be too late then, won't it?'

He shook his head. 'Not if it's a nice day. It won't get dark till six. We could go for a short walk—unless you'll be too tired?'

She thought of her feet at the end of a busy day walking backwards and forwards on the ward, and wondered how many miles she would already have covered by the time she finished. Several, she was sure.

'It depends on what you consider short. My father's idea of a short walk is about twenty minutes of steady strolling. My mother's is two hours at a brisk pace with a pair of Labradors at her heels. Define, please!'

He chuckled. 'Somewhere between the two? An hour of brisk strolling?'

She laughed at him. 'How can you stroll briskly?' she asked, and he grinned and hugged her.

'Don't know. We'll find out.'

He looked down into her eyes, and then his smile faded and something warm and tender took its place. 'Oh, Allie,' he murmured, and then he kissed her. It was a gentle kiss, subtle and restrained, and after a few moments he lifted his head, sighed and tucked her under his chin, holding her close.

She could hear the steady beat of his heart, and it made her feel safe and comforted.

Not that she needed comforting, she thought vaguely, but he seemed to do it anyway, and she decided she could stand any amount of it. After a moment he dropped a kiss on the top of her head and moved away, holding her at arm's length.

'Tea?' he suggested, and she nodded.

'Please.'

'Make yourself at home, I'll be back in a minute. The first job is to find mugs in the kitchen and unearth the kettle. I'll try not to be too long.'

He went out, and she took her first good look around. It was a typical single study bedroom such as you would find in any university halls of residence or hospital accommodation, she thought. Cream walls, indeterminate print curtains, basic and indestructible fitted furniture in pale wood finish, a little *en suite* shower and loo in the corner.

Nothing flashy, but that wasn't what interested her. What she wanted to see was the contents, the personal items that made it *his* room. Things like the books arranged in a neat row on the shelf over the desk.

Medical textbooks, for the most part, of course, but also others, books on mediaeval architecture, stately homes, gardening, well-thumbed paperbacks—thrillers, forensic detectives, the odd classic.

Eclectic taste, she thought, flicking through a couple of them. She put them back and looked at the rest of the room. It was tidy—amazing, considering he was a man, she thought. Most young men she'd met had been total rodents. They'd reminded her of the way her hamster used to organise its cage, when she was a child. Sawdust flicked everywhere, food stashed in odd corners, and the bedding dragged every which way.

He was a definite improvement on Timmy Squeaker, she thought with a chuckle.

She was tempted to open drawers and look for further clues to his personality, but she didn't. Apart from the fact that she wouldn't want him doing it to her, she didn't think she'd find anything. He was too open, too up-front for secrets.

He just wasn't that sort of man.

So she sat on the bed, and settled herself in the corner against the walls with the pillow tucked behind her back, and waited patiently for him to return. He wasn't long, and he'd managed to find two matching mugs, as he was at pains to point out to her.

'Not easy in this place. I'm afraid there's never any milk, so it's instant tea—is that OK?'

'Fine.' She took her mug, and the chocolate digestive he offered her, and dunked it.

'You dunk everything,' he said in fascinated disgust.

'Only biscuits and mints. I'm quite discriminating, really.'

He chuckled and settled down beside her, the biscuits on his lap, and they munched and sipped and she thought, How homely and domestic and settled.

It was a weird feeling, especially since they weren't really settled at all.

She had three biscuits—at least two more than she should have done, she told herself—and then he took her mug out of her hand, put it down on the bedside shelf and gave her a considering look.

'I could take advantage of you, curled up there on my bed looking delectable with that ring of chocolate round your mouth.'

She licked her lips instantly, and then immediately regretted it, because his eyes zeroed in on the action and flickered with heat. 'Hell, woman, don't do that,' he said in a raw, gravelly voice, and drew her into his arms. 'I don't think you have the slightest idea what you do to me, do you?' he murmured, and then promptly showed her.

By the time he lifted his head she was under no illusions.

Furthermore, it was mutual, and he looked down into her eyes and groaned. 'Don't look at me like that,' he pleaded. 'It's difficult enough without you undermining my resolve with those great big baby blues.'

She swallowed a little whimper of frustration, and struggled to sit up. Her hair was on end, her jumper was askew from sliding down the bed and she felt rumpled and wanton.

She caught a glimpse of herself in the mirror opposite and groaned. She *looked* rumpled and wanton. Oh, knickers. She finger-combed her hair straight, and Mark pulled her hands down and picked up a comb and slowly removed the tangles, one by one.

'I love your hair,' he said softly, gliding the comb through the smooth strands as he finished. 'It's like silk. I have fantasies about it spread all over my pillow.'

She looked at him with eyes that must have been all too revealing, and with a groan he shifted her, laying her down so her head was on his pillow. Then, strand by strand, he combed it out in a fan around her head and then sat and looked at her.

'Do you have any idea how much I want to make love to you?' he asked softly, and a tiny whimper rose in her throat and betrayed her.

'Don't, sweetheart,' he murmured. 'Please don't. I don't want it to be a trivial thing when it happens.'

Trivial? Was he crazy? There was so much love welling up inside her she was in danger of bursting, and he thought their lovemaking would be trivial? She swallowed the wall of emotion that was rising in her chest and threatening to choke her, and sat up.

'This is silly,' she said, pulling her hair back and fishing in her bag for a scrunchie to tie it out of the way. 'I ought to go.'

'Yes, I think you should. Thanks for coming with me today to see the house.'

She managed a smile, the screaming wild cat subsiding to a whimpering kitten under her ruthless command. 'My pleasure. It was lovely—I wouldn't have missed it for the world. And thanks for the lunch. Are you really going to do the pantomime?'

He gave a strangled chuckle. 'I don't know. Possibly. It could be fun.'

She arched a disbelieving brow. 'Oh, yeah? All that "Oh, no it isn't" and "Oh, yes it is" stuff? You must be nuts.'

He smiled. 'Very likely.' He tucked an escaping strand of hair behind her ear and sighed. 'Come on. I'll walk you home, it's got dark now and I don't like you walking about out there in the dark.'

Allie laughed. 'How on earth do you think I get home at night in the winter? Taxi? It's about a two-minute walk—not even that. I'm quite safe.'

He made a sceptical noise, and pulled on his jacket. 'Whatever, I'm walking you home. I was brought up to be a gentleman, and you'll just have to put up with that, I'm afraid.'

She didn't mind. It meant another few minutes in his company, and she would have been happy to spend the rest of the day with him. She hesitated on her doorstep, wondering whether to invite him in and offer him supper again, but then she heard Lucy and Beth laughing and thought better of it. They'd give him the third degree, and pull her fingernails after he'd gone for extra little tit-bits.

Better not.

He put his hands on her shoulders and smiled down at her. 'Don't ask me in. I need a cold shower, not your friends' curiosity.'

She chuckled. 'I'd just come to that conclusion myself. I'll see you tomorrow after I finish work—shall I come to you when I'm changed?'

'Good idea. I'll see you tomorrow.'

He brushed his lips over hers, hesitated and then kissed her again, a slow, lingering kiss full of promise.

'Sleep tight,' he murmured, and turning on his heel, he strode away across the street towards the hospital, the lights gleaming on his hair and touching it with gold.

She missed him already.

He turned at the corner and smiled and waved, and she waved back and let herself in, feeling a little lost.

'Hey, it's the prodigal daughter—where've you been? Out with *him?*'

She flapped a hand at Beth and dropped down at the table in the kitchen. 'Is the kettle on?'

'Depends,' Lucy said.

'On?'

'If you'll tell all.'

'There's nothing to tell,' she protested, but they both rolled their eyes and laughed, and Beth grabbed the little mirror that was propped over the sink heater and slapped it in front of her.

Her lips were rosy and her eyes were sparkling and something strange seemed to have happened to her skin, so that it seemed to glow from within. She put the mirror down and sighed.

'Well?' Beth said, pulling out another chair and plopping down in it eagerly. 'What's going on?'

She shrugged. 'We went house-hunting.'

'Blimey, that was quick,' Lucy said. 'How long have you known him?'

'Five years? Five days? And no, it wasn't that sort of house-hunting. Not for *us*, for *him*. He was looking at a couple of cottages.'

'Oh.' Lucy's face fell.

'Find anything?' Beth asked.

'Yes—a lovely little cottage. It's gorgeous.'

'Excellent. So you'll have somewhere private to go.'

Allie laughed awkwardly. 'That's not why he's buying it.'

'Maybe not, but it's a definite perk.'

'Beth, you're impossible. Not everyone wants to go somewhere private with their dates all the time.'

'You want to do it in public?'

'Do what?' she asked innocently.

'Whatever you've been doing all afternoon that's given you whisker burn and bruised lips and that glazed look in your eyes,' Lucy said, shoving the mirror at her again. 'Allie, it's OK. You're allowed. Welcome to the real world.'

'I love him,' she said abruptly, looking up at her friends with eyes that suddenly couldn't see quite so clearly. 'Isn't that crazy? I hardly know him, but I love him, and the worst thing about it is we've got no future together.'

'Not this GP thing?' Beth said disgustedly. 'Allie, you're mad. He's the most gorgeous thing to happen to the hospital in years, and you don't think you've got a future because he's going to work in a surgery and not in Theatre? What are you after? A consultant surgeon with a hefty private practice?'

Allie was horrified. 'It's not like that! It's nothing to do with money. It's the job.'

'It's a fine job. It's a good job.'

'It's awful. I've watched my parents deal with it for the last twenty-three years, don't forget. There's nothing you can tell me about general practice that I don't already know first hand—and I know I can't hack it. There's no point in trying.'

'Even for Mark?'

Lucy looked stunned, and Allie shrugged wretchedly. 'I don't know. I don't know what to do. I can see where it's leading, and I want to go there, but I know my heart's just going to get trashed.'

'Not necessarily. I should go for it,' Beth advised. 'Don't think about his career or yours or the future. Just go with what's happening to you now—that's what matters. The future might never get here, and if it does, you might find you don't want him to be a part of it after all. How will you know if you don't try?'

She wouldn't. He might be unspeakably difficult to live with, or become jealous and possessive and start trying to persuade her to give up her job. He might be a womaniser. He might, of course, be absolutely perfect, but she realised she didn't know him well enough to judge—and she certainly didn't know him well enough to throw herself into an affair with him quite so soon.

'Has that kettle boiled yet?' she asked, changing the subject firmly. 'I could murder a cup of tea.'

She found Jayne in the playroom the following morning, with her older daughter Sheridan, and Claudia, still cheerful despite the treatment for her chest infection.

'Still haven't had that baby, then?' she said with a smile, and Jayne gave a wry laugh.

'Tell me about it. It seems to be going on for ever. Still, only two weeks now, and I'm not complaining, not after all the problems I've had. You know it's my ninth pregnancy?' she told Allie quietly.

Allie shook her head in disbelief. 'I knew you'd had problems, but—so many?'

Jayne smiled wistfully. 'Sometimes I can't believe this isn't all a nasty joke. I keep waiting to wake up and find I've lost it, so, no, I'm not complaining that I'm still pregnant. I'm just looking forward to the birth, so I can believe it's real, but even then the suspense won't be over for a while. We have to have the CF tests done before we can relax.' Her eyes swivelled to the girls, and noticed Claudia looking for a piece of jigsaw puzzle.

'It's gone, Mum,' she said plaintively. 'It's the last bit.'

'Claudia, it's over there, darling. Next to the table.'

Claudia looked in vain, and in the end Jayne stood up. 'I'll get it,' she said, and took a step forwards towards the piece of jigsaw.

'Jayne, I'll pick it up,' Allie offered, just as Claudia darted forwards and grabbed it.

'Got it!' she said, and Jayne turned.

Afterwards Allie couldn't say quite what had happened, but for some reason Jayne's legs seemed to disappear from under her, and with a startled cry she fell headlong across the floor, landing on her side with a tremendous crash.

That's what they mean by heavily pregnant, she thought with a wince, and rushed to Jayne's side. 'Are you all right?' she asked. 'Don't move for a minute, just lie there. Don't forget to breathe—nice, steady breaths. Well done. Claudia, Sheridan, look after your mum. She's all right, she's just had a bump. Just hold her hands while I go and get someone to help her.'

She left the two little girls gripping Jayne's hands like there was no tomorrow, and shot out into the ward. 'Anna, help me, Jayne's gone over.'

'I thought I heard a crash. I was just coming to investigate. Is she all right?'

'I don't know. The girls are with her. She looks pretty shaken.'

They went back in and knelt down beside the pale, trembling woman. 'It's all right, Jayne,' Anna said soothingly. 'Don't worry, my love, we'll soon have you comfy. Allie, can you page Maternity and get someone over here? Who's your consultant, Jayne?'

'Mr Armitage,' she whispered. 'Oh, I do hurt.'

'It's all right, Mummy,' Claudia said calmly, gripping her hand. 'Just breathe nice and slowly—that's it. It's going to be all right, Mummy, the baby's going to be all right. Don't worry. I'm here.'

Allie and Anna exchanged stunned looks. Like mother, like daughter, Allie thought. She'd heard just those words from Jayne to Claudia when she was having her long line in—and now Claudia was comforting Jayne. It brought a huge lump to her throat and clogged her breath for a long moment.

She swallowed hard.

'Girls, do you want to go with Allie and see if you can find your mum a blanket and a pillow?' Anna suggested. 'We'll make her a bit more comfy.'

The girls hung back, clearly reluctant to leave their mother, and Allie held her hands out.

'Come on, girls. Claudia? Sheridan? Let's get the blankets quickly so she isn't cold.'

'I'll stay with her,' Claudia said firmly. 'She needs me. It's all right, Mummy. I'm here. You'll be all right. The baby's going to be OK.'

Allie hesitated for a moment, still marvelling at the role reversal her mother's fall had generated, then shrugged. Claudia was in control of the situation, comforting her mother when until then it had been the other way round. They probably both needed it.

Blinking away sudden tears, Allie took Sheridan and went to phone the Maternity SHO. She bumped into Ben Lazaar as he came onto the ward and heaved a sigh of relief. 'Ben, could you go into the playroom and have a look at Claudia's mum, please?' she asked him. 'She's had a fall.'

'Sure.'

He switched direction without a pause, closed the playroom door behind him and left Allie alone with Sheridan. 'Now, blankets,' she said with a smile.

'Is she OK?' Sheridan asked worriedly, looking back at the door.

'Yes, I'm sure she will be. She's just a bit heavy at the moment to fall over, and she went down with quite a bump. I expect she'll have a few bruises to show you tomorrow. Ah, here's Pearl. Could you be a love and help Sheridan find blankets and pillows for her mum? She's fallen over in the dayroom.'

Pearl's eyes registered dismay, but she took the girl under her wing and ushered her off, chattering happily, and Allie went to the desk and paged Joe Armitage's SHO.

'Mr Armitage is in this morning—would you like him to come over?' the SHO said.

'Good idea, as she fell on hospital property. Would you ask him to come as quickly as possible? I'd hate anything else to happen.'

Within moments he was there, kneeling down beside her and smiling at the children. 'Hi, girls. You looking after Mum?'

They nodded, and he turned to Jayne. 'What have you been doing? I don't know, I turn my back on you for a moment and you throw yourself on the floor.'

'Is the baby all right?' Claudia asked with thinly veiled anxiety.

'I don't know. Let's listen. Anybody checked for anything else?'

Ben nodded. 'I've given her a quick once-over. Nothing obvious apart from nasty bruising. I haven't tried for a heartbeat yet. I was just about to do it.'

So now it was just a question of letting Joe look at her and listen to the baby, and then hopefully they could all relax. Until he got that heartbeat, though, they'd all be in suspense.

He pulled up her blouse a little way, eased down the top of her trousers and put a midwife's baby trumpet against her tummy. A broad smile lit his face, and he nodded. 'Still going strong,' he said calmly. 'Anyone want to listen?'

'Me,' Claudia said firmly, and took the trumpet. A moment later the tension seemed to go out of her. 'See, Mummy, I told you the baby would be all right,' she said reassuringly.

Joe laughed. 'Seems fine. Right, what about Mum herself? How did you land?'

'On my side—and I'm well padded, so it should be all right. My arm hurts, though. I think I landed on a brick.'

'Ouch. OK, let's have you in Maternity and run a check on you from end to end, make sure you get all your bumps looked at and make you more comfortable. Can you get up, or do you want us to put you on a stretcher?'

'I'll get up,' she said, and slowly, very carefully, she eased herself to her feet, allowing Joe and Ben to help her up.

Claudia relaxed again, but only until her mother was put into a wheelchair. Then Joe said, 'Right, let's take you up to Maternity and give you the works.' He pushed her towards the door, and a look of panic flitted across Claudia's face.

'You are coming back, aren't you?' she asked, her voice edged with apprehension. 'The baby will be all right, won't it? Do you want me to come?'

'No, I'll be back,' Jayne promised with a big smile. 'You were right. I'm fine. You and Sheridan stay here and do a puzzle or something. Is it all right if Sheridan stays?' she asked Allie as a worried afterthought.

'It's fine,' Allie assured her firmly. 'Don't worry. You just go and get yourself sorted out—'

'I need to ring George—'

'I'll do it. Go. Don't fret. He can contact you up in Maternity.'

She smiled tiredly, blew a kiss to the children and was wheeled away. Sheridan hugged Claudia, and Allie ushered them back to Claudia's bedside. It was time for her next pre-gent test, and she hoped it wouldn't be too traumatic.

Yet again, though, she was stunned by the child's emotional resources. Even without her mother's support, she was fine, and her sister was entrusted with the job of holding her other hand.

It was astonishing, Allie thought as she ran home

to change before her walk with Mark, how close and supportive a family could be.

Astonishing and humbling. She dragged on her jeans and good, strong trainers, pulled a snuggly fleece over her head and ran back to the hospital to Mark's room, knocking impatiently on his door. 'Mark?' she called, and knocked again, suddenly unable to wait to see him, to drive out the image of Claudia, so small, so brave, comforting her mother.

He opened his door and took one look at her before pulling her into his arms. 'Allie? Whatever's wrong?' he asked.

'It's Claudia,' she said, and burst into tears.

CHAPTER FIVE

MARK was stunned. Claudia? What about Claudia?
He drew Allie into his room, sat down on the bed and
held her while she howled.

They must have lost the little girl, he thought, and
couldn't understand it. What had gone wrong?
Although goodness knows she had enough strikes
against her, what with the long line, the chest infection, the gastrostomy tube—to say nothing of the CF
itself.

But the last time he'd seen her, she'd been fine.
Nothing out of the way, and she'd been making progress with her chest.

'What happened?' he asked when Allie hiccupped
to a halt.

She sniffed and scrubbed her nose on a tissue and
shook her head. 'Jayne had a fall, and Claudia was
brilliant. She held her hand and talked to her, and told
her it was going to be all right—she's just got such
guts—'

She bit her lip and sniffed again, and Mark hugged
her, relieved beyond reason that there was nothing
wrong with Claudia. 'How's Jayne now?'

'Up in Maternity. She seems to be fine, but she's
very shaken and bruised. She went down with such a
crash, Mark—I watched her fall, and I couldn't see
how it happened. She didn't trip—she just—went. It
was awful. Ben looked at her, and Joe Armitage came
down and checked her over and whisked her off, and

83

I gather she and the baby are fine, but poor Claudia and Sheridan look so lost without her.'

Her chin started to wobble again, and he quickly got her back to basics. 'Did you have to fill in an accident report?'

Allie rolled her eyes. 'Did I! I was the only one there, other than the children, and the paperwork took ages. I got hardly anything done after she fell.' She sat up straighter and gave an embarrassed little smile. 'Still, all done now. I'm sorry about that—I just felt so proud of her and so humble.'

'I know.' He hugged her again, dropped a kiss on each of her damp, pink eyes and told her to wash her face. She disappeared into his little bathroom, and he pulled on a jumper, picked up his coat and boots and smiled at her as she emerged, damp but a little more composed.

'All set?'

She nodded, and he slung his arm round her shoulders and led her to his car. Poor Allie. It must have been a shock watching Jayne fall and being so helpless.

'It's a gorgeous day,' she murmured. 'I hadn't even noticed.'

He chuckled. 'I had. I've been itching to get out here—I forced myself to do some studying, but it was touch and go. I went for a stroll at lunchtime and nearly didn't come back!'

He ushered her into his car and shut the door, then slid behind the wheel. He didn't need his coat at the moment, and in fact it was so mild now he couldn't believe how cold it had been the previous week in the evenings.

That was autumn for you, though, he thought. It

was his favourite time of year, with the leaves turning that stunning red-gold and the days crisp and bright. The road to Pulham wound through another little village on the way, with pretty cottages and little streams and horses grazing peacefully, and he shrugged off the hours of study and the noise of the town traffic and let the beauty of the countryside flow over him and enjoyed Allie's quiet company.

Then they were in Pulham, going down the lane past Church Cottage, and he felt a surge of something that could have been homecoming. Mrs Pettitt was standing in the garden with a man of about forty, probably her son, and he pulled over and got out.

'Good afternoon,' he called, and she peered at him and then smiled broadly.

'Dr Jarvis—how lovely to see you. You haven't changed your mind?' she added anxiously, and he laughed and shook his head.

'Not a chance.'

'Oh, good. Minnie will be pleased. Gerald, this is Dr Jarvis who's buying my cottage. You spoke to him yesterday, didn't you? Dr Jarvis, my son Gerald.'

They shook hands over the gate, and Mrs Pettitt asked him in.

He refused, a little reluctantly, and explained that he and Allie were going for a walk while it was still light, to explore the area.

'Come for tea afterwards, then,' she suggested. 'I've got a bit of fruitcake left, and some homemade raspberry jam. Did I show you the raspberry canes in the garden?'

He shook his head and laughed. 'We didn't look outside properly. Perhaps we'll explore it later, once we've had a walk. Tea would be lovely, thanks.'

'About an hour?'

He nodded. 'Something like that, unless we get lost.'

'You won't,' Gerald told him. 'The paths are clearly marked. Mother's got a map—hang on, I'll get it for you. We use it sometimes when we come over with the children.'

So he and Allie set off, armed with the borrowed map, and strolled briskly through the woods and along beside the stream, and Allie laughed and showered him with autumn leaves, and he kissed her, in the peaceful stillness in the middle of the wood, and thought how lucky he would be to live here.

All he needed was for nothing to go wrong between now and completion of the sale, and the cottage would be his. He could picture it, with Allie pottering about in socks and jeans and a baggy old jumper, making tea while he dug the garden and chased Minnie off the bird table—

'Penny for them.'

He looked down into her eyes and smiled. 'I was just daydreaming about the cottage.'

She glanced at her watch. 'Talking of which, Mrs Pettitt will be expecting us. We ought to get back.'

He nodded, but he didn't move. It felt so good holding her in his arms. He kissed her again, then once more for good measure, then groaned softly and rocked her against his chest. 'This is driving me crazy,' he murmured.

'So stop doing it,' she said with a laugh.

'No. Don't want to.'

She chuckled and ducked out of his arms. 'Tough. I want tea and cake—last one there's a sissy.'

He chased her through the woods, marvelling at her

quickness and sure-footedness, until she caught her foot in a root and went flying. She wasn't hurt, just winded and still laughing, and he kissed her again, right there on the ground.

If it hadn't been for the Labrador sniffing around them a few moments later, the dog's owners might have fallen over them, he thought, pulling Allie to her feet and brushing leaves from her clothes and hair.

She looked beautiful, tousled and warm from their walk, her lips rosy from kissing him and her eyes sparkling with happiness.

At least, he hoped it was happiness. It might just have been the sting of the wind.

It had been another wonderful day, Allie thought. The walk had been lovely, the cottage was even prettier than she remembered, and Minnie had spent their whole visit curled up on her lap flexing her claws in Allie's knee and dribbling.

She hadn't really minded. Mrs Pettitt had told her she was honoured, but she was at a loss to know quite how. Her knee was flayed, her jeans were soggy and the cat had mugged her for her cake, but apart from that she was fine, and at least the cat seemed to like her!

And then Mark had taken her back to his room and kissed her until she thought her knees would dissolve and she'd never walk again. It had been bad enough in the woods, but in the privacy of his room with no one to disturb them, they'd lain on the bed in the dark and he'd driven her mad with his lips and hands and the gentle pressure of his body against hers.

Finally he'd curled her into his shoulder and hugged her against him, and she'd drifted off to sleep,

waking now, some time later, to the realisation that it
was after midnight and she was still in his room, on
his bed, in his arms.

'Mark?' She shook him gently, rousing him from
a deep sleep. He mumbled something and pulled her
firmly into his arms, thrusting one solid, heavy thigh
between hers and rolling against her.

'Mark,' she repeated, shaking his shoulder again
and resisting the urge to snuggle deeper into his embrace and stay there. She groped for the bedside light
and switched it on, shaking him again.

'Mmm,' he mumbled. 'Wazamatta?'

'Mark, I have to go home.'

His eyes opened, and slowly he focused on her.
'What time is it?' he asked, bemused.

'Nearly twelve-thirty.'

'Good. Don't have to get up yet.'

She laughed and pushed him again. 'I do. I have
to go home.'

He woke up then, studied her thoughtfully and said,
very softly, 'You don't have to. You could stay.'

His meaning was quite clear. It was part of his
'let's see what happens' philosophy, but suddenly she
didn't want to. It seemed—not cold-blooded, exactly,
but rather the reverse, just something they would drift
into without any commitment or forethought, and she
wanted more than that.

She let her breath out on a sigh, and he smiled
ruefully. 'Is that a no?'

'Yes. I mean, yes, it's a no. I'm sorry—'

'Don't be. I'm glad. I'm tired, we both have to go
to work in the morning—that's not good enough for
our first time.' He kissed her again, just gently, a
slightly regretful kiss, and then rolled away from her

and stood up, pulling her to her feet. 'Come on, I'll walk you back.'

'You don't need to,' she protested, but he shook his head.

'I do. I wouldn't sleep a wink if I just let you go at this time of night.'

'You fuss too much—you're like my mother.'

'Dear lady. How is she?'

Allie laughed. 'She's fine. She keeps asking when I'm going to take you over there so they can see you again.'

'Any time you like,' he said with a smile. 'They're lovely people. I'd be happy to see them again.'

'I'll tell her that.'

She slipped on her shoes, shrugged into her coat and walked with him out into the cold, clear night. It was crisp and frosty, and their breath misted in little huffs on the air. He snuggled her close, and in the shelter of her porch he kissed her again.

'I must be mad to let you go,' he murmured against her hair, and then straightened with a ragged sigh. 'Go on, go inside. I'll see you in the morning.'

She went, thinking that she must be mad to *let* him let her go, and lay in her bed thinking about him and the feel of his body warm and solid against hers, and missed him.

'So, what's new?' she asked Anna.

'Since yesterday? Jayne's all right—she just had some horrible bruises, but nothing too drastic. Claudia's very pleased to see her again, anyway. I think she was afraid Jayne would lose the baby.'

'Mmm. She said.'

'And we've had a six-year-old in who was playing

on a ladder while her father's back was turned and
the ladder slipped and she's broken her arm. She had
surgery last night when she came in, because it was
a nasty greenstick fracture of her radius and ulna and
her hand was tingling and going blue. Another appendix, two babies with colicky pain and vomiting
and a riding accident for observation following a head
injury.'

'Just another average Sunday, then,' Allie said with
a smile. 'How's Darren?'

'Picking up nicely. They're going to send him
home for a while and let his mother do the suppositories—he'll love that! Still, he'll be happier at home.
He goes at lunchtime, I think. And apart from the
scheduled pre-ops that came in yesterday afternoon,
that's all. So how was the rest of your Sunday?'

'Lovely,' she said truthfully. 'A walk in the coun-
try, tea and fruitcake with a delightful elderly lady
and a quiet evening in.'

In with Mark, but Anna didn't have to know that.
She was looking envious as it was!

Allie didn't see Mark until later, and then he was
on the phone in the office and waved a hand wildly
to indicate she should stay. She slipped out and made
two mugs of tea and brought them back, then settled
herself in the corner while he finished his conversation.

She could only hear one side, but it was something
to do with the house, and when he put the phone
down he was smiling. 'That's that organised,' he said
in satisfaction. 'The survey is being carried out in the
next couple of days, and if all's well I should be able
to take the house over as soon as Mrs Pettitt is ready.'

'Are you going to move in straight away?' Allie

asked, suddenly aware that he wouldn't be in the hospital and she wouldn't be able to just amble over the road and find him. Even in just a week, she'd grown used to the thought of him being so close.

'Yes—but I'll still keep the room here on. I need somewhere for when I'm on call, and when the plumbing's up the Swanee because I've ripped out all the pipes or whatever. Why, will you miss me?' he asked in a teasing voice, and she wondered what he wanted to hear. Oh, well, it might as well be the truth.

'Yes,' she said honestly. 'Yes, I will.'

The smile faded from his face, replaced by something tender and understanding. 'I'm on call tonight,' he said. 'Otherwise I'd take you out for dinner.'

'I don't need another big meal. I'll get fat.'

'We could have a take-away in my room.'

'How is that less fattening?'

He laughed. 'It isn't, but you don't need to lose weight.'

'I don't need to gain it, either.'

'So I'll go to the supermarket and buy loads of salads and you can sit in the corner and gnaw carrots and lettuce.'

She wrinkled her nose at the thought. 'I could feed you at my house—your bleep works over there.'

He shook his head. 'I'll just have to leave in the middle. Don't worry. I'll wade through another couple of textbooks from the library in between calls.'

'Just think how much worse it'll be when you're a GP. At least here you only have to toddle down the corridor.'

He smiled and stood up. 'It won't work, Allie. I know what I want.' He came over to her and dropped a kiss on her lips. 'Thanks for the tea. I'll see you later. I have to go down to the clinic.'

He went out, leaving her feeling unaccountably depressed. He was obviously not going to be persuaded to give up the idea of general practice, she realised, and that left her in the unenviable position of falling head over heels for a man she couldn't allow herself to love.

Damn.

She scrubbed away the sudden tears and stood up impatiently. She was being silly. It was a very slight romance, not the love of the century. She ought to remember that.

She went back out onto the ward, just as one of the post-ops came back down from Theatre. Good. Just what she needed—plenty to do. She went and busied herself with the little girl, and chatted to the mother, and forced Mark Jarvis and his all-too-tempting kisses to the back of her mind.

'How's your mum?' Allie asked Claudia the following morning as she checked her long line and flushed it with Hepsal to keep it clear.

'Fine. She had the baby last night in Pizza Hut.'

Allie nearly dropped the syringe. 'She *what!* You're joking!'

'Yeah, that's right. I'm joking.'

Claudia doubled up giggling, and Allie joined in ruefully. 'You little minx. How is she really?'

'Oh, fine. She's going to have it on Wednesday— that's tomorrow. She told us last night. She and Daddy took me and Sheridan out for dinner and told us. Isn't it exciting? I can't believe we're really going to have a baby—not after last time.'

Allie perched on the edge of the bed. 'Were you very sad last time?' she asked gently.

Her huge blue eyes were sober in her little face. 'When the baby died? Yes. Mummy was very sad, too. It was awful. I can't believe it's going to be all right. Mummy says it might have CF and they won't know till it's born. I hope it doesn't, but if it does, it won't be so bad. It can keep me company.'

Claudia first, CF second, Allie thought to herself, remembering what Jayne had told her. The disease had always been kept firmly in the background, not allowed to dominate their lives despite the huge impact it inevitably had. And it seemed it had worked, because clearly Claudia didn't think it was anything too terrible to worry about. After all, she had CF and she was all right.

Allie could have cried. Instead she finished flushing the line, cleared up all the debris and stood up.

'Right, that's you sorted,' she said.

'I wonder if it'll be a boy or a girl?' Claudia murmured.

'You'll know soon,' she said. 'Only another day or so and it'll be here. That's something to look forward to, isn't it?'

'I will be able to go up and see her on Maternity, won't I?' she asked anxiously. 'I mean, after she has the baby?'

'Of course, love,' Allie reassured her, sitting down and giving her a hug. 'Just the moment she's allowed visitors, we'll be up there. I'll take you myself, because I'm a sucker for tiny babies. OK?'

Claudia nodded, her long blonde hair bobbing gently round her face. 'OK. Can I go and have breakfast now?'

'Sure. Don't forget your pills.'

'I won't,' she said, old beyond her years, and skipped off, looking for all the world like a normal seven-year-old.

Which, of course, she was, Allie reminded herself, and went off deep in thought to clear away the debris and check the stock in the treatment room.

Mark walked up behind her when she was in there and put his hands on her waist and made her jump. She gave a little scream and then giggled, slapping his hands away and wagging her finger at him.

'I nearly died of fright,' she chided.

He grinned, a slow, sexy, lazy grin that did terrible things to her pulse. 'Sorry,' he said, totally unrepentant.

'You obviously weren't working hard enough last night,' she said repressively, and he gave a wry laugh.

'Are you kidding? I didn't get to bed at all. I've got the afternoon off, though—want to sleep with me?'

She did. She could think of nothing more wonderful than curling up in his arms and going to sleep. However she had work to do, and her sanity to protect.

'Sorry, you'll have to sleep by yourself this time,' she said, just as Anna came in.

Her colleague blinked, apologised and went out again, looking more curious than ever, and Allie rolled her eyes and laughed. 'How do I get out of that?' she asked.

He shrugged. 'Why bother? Unless you're ashamed of anyone thinking we're having that sort of a relationship.'

What a loaded question! 'Not ashamed, exactly,'

she corrected. 'I just don't need the third degree off Anna—or my housemates, and they're all as bad as each other. Insatiably curious and desperate to get me matched up with somebody. Actually they're worse than my mother!'

He chuckled. 'They can't be worse than *my* mother. She's a nightmare. She's desperate to be a grandmother. That's what you get for being an only child.'

'Well, at least I don't get that,' Allie said gratefully. 'My older brother's engaged to a very nice girl, and that's kept them quiet for a bit.'

'Be thankful for small mercies,' he advised her, and cocked his head on one side, ignoring his bleep for a moment. 'Are you sure I can't talk you into snuggling up for a little kip later?'

If he'd had the slightest idea how tempted she was, he wouldn't have given in, but he obviously didn't, because he took her laughing refusal at face value, gave an exaggerated sigh and went out, blowing her a kiss.

Anna was in through the door before the air had stopped moving. Allie shot her a warning look. 'Just don't ask,' she said warningly, and Anna rolled her eyes.

'You tell him—on the ward, in my hearing—that he'll have to sleep by himself tonight, and expect me not to ask? You're a hard woman.'

Allie gave a wry chuckle. 'It wasn't what it sounded like.'

Anna cocked a brow. 'You're telling me you turned down an invitation to sleep with that man and it wasn't what it sounded like? What on earth *was* it, then? Sleep therapy?'

Allie laughed, and shook her head. 'Forget it, Anna. Anyway, aren't we busy?'

'Like you wouldn't believe. Actually I was looking for you. We've got a child coming in with febrile convulsions following an ear infection—he's two, he's been fitting and unless I'm mistaken they've just called Mark down to A&E to see him. He's going to be coming to us under sedation, and we may have to have him on a ventilator if they have to paralyse him to stop the fits. Can you get a cot ready?'

'Sure.' Allie was already walking towards the door, mentally cataloguing the things she'd need. 'Is Mum staying?'

'Don't know. Go for a cubicle anyway—we want peace and quiet. He'll need specialling—will you do it, please?'

She nodded again, went to the mercifully empty little family room near the nurses' station and re-moved the patient's bed, replacing it with a large cot. They wouldn't want a convulsing child in a bed, even with cot sides, and if he was still small enough to fit in the cot, then in the cot he'd be.

She set up the monitoring equipment, checked the ventilator was working in case it was needed and made up the cot with the help of another nurse. Then the baby arrived, sedated now and no longer fitting, with Mark in attendance quietly issuing instructions and working on the child.

He was linked up to the piped oxygen, the monitor leads were attached to him and he was uncovered except for the nappy. 'He's on antibiotics IV to sort that ear infection and bring down his temperature, and in the meantime he needs sponging constantly until

his temperature falls below thirty-eight degrees C.
Are you specialling him?'

Allie nodded, and Mark smiled slightly. 'Good.
Mum's staying, I believe—is that right, Carol?'

The panic-stricken woman nodded. 'If that's all
right?'

'Of course it is. The bed's always made up in here,'
Allie said, 'so it's no problem. It's a bit short,
though—it's a child's bed, to save space, but I expect
you'll be able to manage. You aren't very tall, are
you?'

She shook her head. 'I'll be fine. I'm not worried
about me, just Toby. Is he going to be all right now?'
she asked anxiously.

'I believe so,' Mark assured her. 'He just needs
time. We'll get his temperature down, let him settle
and assess him again later. I should think by tomorrow he'll be sitting up and chatting to you.'

Allie thought the mother was going to burst into
tears at the very thought. She sniffed, nodded and
thanked him, and he smiled at her and went out, winking at Allie over her head.

He looks tired, she thought. Tired enough to drop.
Would he eat properly? Not that he was thin, and
sleep was probably what he needed more than anything. She just wanted to mother him.

She settled little Toby, checked that everything was
working and did his obs, filled in the chart and went
to get Carol a cup of tea. She was still visibly upset,
and had been unable to contact her husband to let him
know what had happened. Allie caught her using a
mobile phone, explained the risk of upsetting delicate
electronic equipment on the wards, such as pethidine

pumps, and sent her outside to use the phone in the car park.

Little Toby was flat out with his sedation, and she checked his nappy, sponged him down on the arms and legs with warm water and watched as his temperature slowly came down from over forty degrees to just over thirty-nine, then gradually over the next couple of hours to just under thirty-nine.

His respiration was a little depressed, of course, because his body had been so relaxed by the sedation in order to stop him fitting. His father arrived, and Allie left him alone with his parents for a little while so they could talk and cuddle him.

'How is he?' Anna asked when Allie went into the office.

'Seems fine. No more fits. He's cooling well, and he looks all right. His colour's improving—he was a bit pale and blue when he arrived on the ward.'

'Good. I've put you down to cover him tomorrow afternoon as well, if he's still here, so hopefully he won't be and I can have you back. We're a bit pushed—oh, and Mark said he's gone back to his room and could you pop in on your way home when you're off duty, please?'

Her heart gave a little leap, and she squashed it firmly. 'Sure,' she said. 'Although I expect he'll be asleep.'

'He said he'd wait up for you.'

He might have said that, Allie thought a couple of hours later as she went off duty, but he'd lied. She tapped lightly, and all she could hear was silence.

She rummaged in her bag for a bit of paper, scribbled a note on it and was about to slide it under the door when it opened to reveal Mark, bleary-eyed, his shirt undone, feet bare, propping up the wall.

'You came,' he said, and she sighed.

'I didn't mean to wake you, but Anna said you wanted to see me?'

His smile was rueful. 'I was going to suggest we went for another walk, but I'm shattered. I'm going to bed. Want to join me?'

'No,' she lied, 'and you should have been there already instead of pretending to stay up.'

'I'd asked Anna to ask you to pop in. It didn't seem fair.'

She went up on tiptoe and kissed him. 'Of course it's fair. You go to bed, and I'll see you tomorrow. I'm on in the afternoon—twelve till nine.'

'OK. I'll see you. Take care.'

She felt his eyes on her all the way down the corridor, and when she glanced back as she turned the corner, he lifted his hand in farewell.

It didn't help. She had an almost overwhelming urge to run back and throw herself into his arms...

CHAPTER SIX

JAYNE'S baby was born early the following afternoon, by which time young Toby was over his convulsions and chattering to his mother and running round the ward being a typical little toddler, his ear infection all but forgotten. To everyone's great relief he seemed to have suffered no side effects and once the ENT physician was happy with his ear, he was going home.

Allie, therefore, was off the hook for specialling him, and was able to go with Jayne's husband and Sheridan and Claudia to Maternity to see the girls' new baby brother. Claudia was both excited and scared all at the same time, and Allie was touched to see her behaving like a child for once. Her maturity was sometimes mind-boggling, but today, like her big sister, she was just an excited little girl seeing her baby brother for the first time.

And then the strain of the past few years showed through, as Claudia looked down at the tiny baby in the cot beside her mother's bed, and said in disbelief, 'Are you *sure* he's really ours?'

'Yes, he really is,' Jayne assured her, and Allie could see the wonder and disbelief on her face as well.

'What's he called?' Allie asked, marvelling yet again at the minute perfection that was a newborn baby.

'Kieran,' Jayne told her. 'After the Audley Town footballer. He's playing tonight—hopefully he'll score. That would be nice, wouldn't it, my sweet-heart?' she crooned, leaning over the cot.

The baby ignored her, busily sleeping after the exhausting business of childbirth, and Sheridan and Claudia peeled back the blanket and counted his fingers and toes, and laughed about his skinny little legs.

Allie winked at Jayne. 'Well done, Mum. Are you OK?'

Jayne nodded, her eyes sparkling with unshed tears. 'Yes, I'm fine. I just don't believe he's here, and alive and well, and everything seems fine.'

Seems fine, Allie thought. Not *is* fine. They still had the blood tests to do, and after a few weeks the sweat test to see if the sodium levels were raised. If not, then they could finally heave a sigh of relief in the knowledge that he was clear of CF, and would live a normal life.

Allie looked at her watch, then at Jayne's husband, supervising the girls as they checked the baby out. 'I have to go back. Could you bring Claudia back to the ward in a little while, or do you want someone to fetch her?'

'I can do it, that's fine,' George said. 'Don't worry. And thanks for coming up.'

Allie laughed. 'No problem. There was no way I'd miss the chance of seeing the baby!'

She dragged herself away after another lingering look, and went quickly back to the ward. Mark was just coming out as she went in, and smiled at her.

'Hi—I gather you've been up to Maternity—how's the new arrival?'

'Gorgeous,' she said wistfully. 'He's lovely. There's just something so perfect about new babies,

I don't know what it is. They're so fragile and yet so tough. Amazing.'

He gave her an indulgent smile. 'I take it you like babies.'

'Oh, yes. My mother's always said she pities my husband, because I'll probably end up with dozens.'

He grinned. 'I can picture you, surrounded by lots of little blond mops at varying heights, all busily colouring or painting or sticking disgusting blobs of pasta on hideous coloured sugar paper—perhaps you should have been a primary school teacher?'

She shuddered. 'Oh, no. I love my job. I'll stick blobs with my own children, but I'd rather get other people's better and send them home!'

He laughed and raised a hand, moving away down the corridor backwards, still talking. 'I have to go— another clinic. I'll see you soon—what time do you finish tonight?'

'Nine,' she told him, 'and I've got washing to sort out and I'm on at seven tomorrow.'

'Yuck. Oh, well, never mind. I was going to suggest going out, but it's going to be too late for you. Another time, then.'

'I thought it was the panto auditions tonight in Pulham?' she said, and he ground to a halt and smacked his forehead.

'Damn. It is. Oh, well, if you can't manage tonight I'll go to that instead. I said I would, so I probably ought to.' He grinned. 'Stand by to meet the new Prince Charming.'

She chuckled. 'More like one of the ugly sisters.'

'Cheeky.' He smiled and waved, and strode off down the corridor whistling softly, hands rammed in his trouser pockets, coat flapping behind him as he ate up the ground with his long stride.

She watched him go, and felt a wave of regret. Still, it was for the best. She didn't really need to keep spending time with him, because she was just getting in deeper and that was a bad idea. Still, there was always the next time.

However, between the way their shifts worked and the fact that Allie was trying—all too successfully—to put some space between them, they hardly saw each other for the rest of that week.

On Friday the Audley Town football team—well, two of them, anyway!—came in to see the kids and raise morale. They often popped in, and the kids were always thrilled to see them, especially the boys on traction who were missing the chance to see their heroes in action.

Claudia was tickled pink when one of them spoke to her, and when she told them that her two-day-old baby brother was called Kieran after one of their number, and he was still in the hospital, they insisted on going to see their team-mate's namesake.

They took Claudia with them, and when she came back she was sparkling and bubbling and completely over the top.

'They were excellent!' she said. 'We all had our photos taken with them and they said we're going to be in the paper! Isn't that amazing?'

Allie hugged her, and thought, not for the first time, that she was feeling a little thinner in the last day or two. 'Sweetheart, I think you need to be linked up to the pump again so we can feed Piglet a bit more in the day as well as at night—what do you think? Are you getting a bit thinner?'

Claudia nodded. 'Maybe. I haven't been especially hungry this week, so eating's been horrid.'

'OK, darling. I'll weigh you and talk to the doctor, and if he thinks it's a good idea we'll put Piglet on the pump for an extra hour or two a day, OK? I'll speak to him now.'

She left Claudia with the others, bragging about her photo-call with the Town players, and contacted Mark. He came up to the ward, checked Claudia's weight record and agreed that she should have an extra two hours of feeding a day through the gastrostomy tube.

It was no problem to Claudia, she just pushed the trolley with the pump and feed on it around with her, and it would give her extra nutrition without her having to make the effort of eating, always a problem with CF children who had to take in such a huge number of calories to keep themselves going. After a while even eating really nice things got boring.

Claudia went off with her trolley as soon as Allie had set the feed up, and she went into the office to find Mark there, perched on the desk cradling the phone in his hand. When she went in he dropped it back on the hook and pressed his palm to his chest. 'Alone at last,' he said theatrically, and she rolled her eyes.

'Hello to you, too. The panto's obviously going to your head.'

He grimaced and laughed softly. 'I'm Sir Prancelot—we're doing some crazy version of King Arthur. Lots of silly innuendo. I seem to be the Buttons character—the one who doesn't get the girl, that everybody feels sorry for.'

'Aaaaahhhhhhhh,' Allie said in true panto style, and he chuckled.

'Don't. I could live to regret it. It's a huge part.'

She laughed at him, fairly kindly. 'Told you you were a mug.'

'I know, I know. It'll be a good chance to meet everyone in the village and break into the community, though.'

'Yes, they'll all think you're a sucker,' she said drily. 'Any news on the house?'

'It's passed the survey—well, the building society want some bits and pieces done in the first six months, but it's all agreed and it looks like I'll take possession next week.'

'Next week?' she exclaimed incredulously. 'As soon as that? It isn't even a week since you saw it!'

'I know. I can't believe it myself. Still, Mrs Pettitt's already gone into her sheltered housing, apparently, and she's got a friend there, so she's settled in well. Her son wants to know if I'd like the bed—apparently they're having difficulty getting it out, and he said they've chucked the mattress but if I want the bed he'll leave it.'

'Is it worth having?' she asked doubtfully, and he shrugged.

'Pass. Could be. It's a double, with heavy wooden ends, and they had to take the window out to get it in, apparently. I said leave it. He didn't want any money for it. I can always saw it up and burn it, if necessary.'

So her idea of taking the furniture upstairs plank by plank wasn't so very far from the truth, then! She tried to picture the bed, and couldn't. 'What's it like?' she asked. 'I don't remember it at all.'

'Nor do I,' he admitted ruefully. 'Still, I don't have long to wait to find out. There's so much I can't remember about the house—I just hope to God I like it when I get to see it again!'

Allie chuckled. 'I'm sure you will. It was lovely. I tell you what, if you don't like it you can swap with me. I'll pay my rent, and you can pay your mortgage, and I'll live there and you can live with Beth and Lucy.'

'Good grief! Would I survive?'

She thought of her friends left alone with all that muscle and sex appeal, and laughed. 'I doubt it. You might die happy, though. Still, I doubt if it will come to that, I'm sure you'll still like the house.'

'Seems almost a shame,' he said musingly, and Allie slapped him on the shoulder with a set of notes and shooed him out of the office.

'Go and do something useful instead of cluttering up the place,' she ordered, and he saluted and headed for the door, then hesitated.

'Before I go—I don't suppose you fancy a trip to visit your parents this weekend? I'd love a chance to chat to your father, if he's about. I've got one or two questions I'd like to ask him if you think he wouldn't mind.'

'I'm sure he'd be delighted,' she said honestly. 'How about lunch on Sunday—why don't you join us? My brother and his fiancée are there for the weekend, but they have to leave straight after lunch, so you could chat to Dad then while Mum and I wash up, if you like. Or you could wash up and talk at the same time, and Mum and I could go and put our feet up with a cup of tea!' she teased.

He gave a wry grunt of laughter. 'That sounds more likely.'

'Want me to ask them?'

'If you would. What are you doing tonight?'

'Working,' she said, wrinkling her nose, 'and tomorrow morning. I've got Sunday off, and Monday and Tuesday morning.'

'I'll book you in advance,' he said with a grin. 'Monday night—damn. I'm on call. How about tomorrow night?'

'I'm going to my parents. I'll be there till Sunday afternoon.'

He sighed. 'Oh, well, I'll see you at your parents' on Sunday for lunch, then, if that's all right. Let me know when you've spoken to them, could you? I'd hate to turn up unannounced.'

He waggled his fingers and left, and for a moment she contemplated running after him and telling him she'd go out with him tomorrow and just see her parents for lunch, but it seemed silly.

Anyway, she was trying to cool things down, not heat them up, and every time they were alone together things got hotter and hotter. It was only a matter of time before the flames flared out of control, she thought, and despite the yearning in her heart, she really, really didn't want to get involved with a GP.

'Oh, dammit,' she muttered, slamming a drawer shut and stomping out into the ward. 'Why does he have to be so darned appealing?'

'You're not talking about our lovely Dr Jarvis, are you?' Anna teased, coming up behind her on silent feet.

She laid her hand on her heart and turned, giving Anna a mock glare. 'Will you lot all stop trying to frighten the daylights out of me?' she said laughingly. 'And yes, I was.'

'If you can't cope, just hand him over,' Anna said, only half jokingly, Allie thought. 'I'll force myself to make do with him.'

'I think I can just about manage,' she said drily, but she wondered if she could, or if this time she'd bitten off more than she could chew…

Sunday lunch was the usual slightly chaotic family affair, with mountains of food to prepare and lots of banter over the kitchen table as they peeled and chopped the vegetables and watched the oven door hungrily.

It was a roast—of course, because Sunday lunch was always a roast—and so there was lots to do. Daniel's fiancée Rosie pitched in with them all, and she was sweet and funny and they all loved her. They'd been discussing the wedding the night before, and since her parents lived in Canada now, they wanted to have the wedding from Daniel's family home.

Allie's mother was thrilled to bits to have a wedding to get her teeth into, and they were throwing ideas around for the reception when the doorbell rang, the dogs leapt up barking wildly and hurled themselves down the hall, and Allie scrambled to her feet and ran after them.

'Bruno, Oscar, stop it!' she yelled. 'Sit!'

They sat, bottoms wriggling, tails lashing at a hundred beats a minute, and she opened the door and let Mark in. 'Hi,' she said, her heart racing faster than the dogs' tails, and he smiled and hugged her.

'Hi yourself. All right?'

'Mmm. Did you find it OK?'

'I know the way,' he reminded her, then looked over her shoulder. 'Kiss me good morning,' he ordered softly, and she went up on tiptoe and pressed her lips to his, just as her father came round the corner of the hall.

'Ah, Mark, welcome. Come on in. How lovely to see you,' he said, taking Mark's hand and shaking it warmly. 'Come down to the kitchen. We're planning Daniel and Rosie's wedding at the moment, and the lunch is sort of under way. Come and join in.'

They went into the kitchen, and Allie's mother wiped her hands on a teatowel, pulled off her pinny and hugged Mark hard. 'How are you?' she asked, holding him by the arms and standing back to study him. 'You look well. Very well. I don't think you met Daniel when you were here, did you? He was in India on his gap year.'

'Don't! That was so long ago,' Daniel said, getting to his feet with a laugh. 'Nice to meet you.'

They all shook hands, and Mrs Baker sat Mark at the table and carried on chopping and talking at once—her forte. 'So, tell me, how are you enjoying the Audley?' she asked over her shoulder.

'Oh, you know—it's another hospital. I like it, as hospitals go, but it can't compete with general practice.'

'Totally different ball game, I quite agree,' her father chipped in. 'Can I get you a sherry?'

'Ah, no, I won't, I'm driving, thanks.'

'Coffee?'

'I'll make it,' Allie said, getting to her feet again and leaving Mark and Daniel to get to know each other.

Very soon the lunch was on the table, and they were all settling down to eat when Mrs Baker said, 'So when do you think this wedding's going to take place? Easter?'

Daniel and Rosie exchanged speaking glances, and Daniel cleared his throat. 'Actually, that might be a bit late,' he said carefully. 'Ah—you see—Rosie's pregnant—the baby's due at the end of May.'

For a moment there was utter, stunned silence, and then all hell broke loose. There was lots of hugging and kissing and laughing and crying, and in a lull Allie shook her head and said, 'How on earth did you manage to do that?'

Daniel went brick-red and rolled his eyes. 'Um— the usual way?' he offered, and Allie swatted him.

'You know what I mean!' she laughed.

'It was actually planned,' Rosie said softly. 'We really want a baby. It was afterwards we thought, if we've got that sort of commitment to each other, we should probably think about being married. It sort of follows.'

'Except that traditionally it follows the other way round,' her prospective father-in-law reminded her gently. 'However, at least you're doing it. And you look well, Rosie,' he said with a smile, 'and you're going to make me a grandfather. What a terrifying thought.'

'I'm going to be an aunt,' Allie said, awestruck. 'How very odd. My brother's going to be a daddy. That's really quite bizarre.'

'Look on the bright side, Alison,' her mother said, 'you'll have a baby to cuddle whenever you see them. You'll like that.'

'We'll have to handcuff it to the cot or she'll pinch it,' Daniel warned Rosie. 'She's nuts about babies.'

She met Mark's eyes over the table and winked at him. 'See?' she mouthed. 'They all tease me.'

He winked back, his eyes crinkling with a smile, and their legs clashed under the table. He apologised, but she kicked off her shoes under the table and found his foot again and slid her toes up inside his trouser leg. His eyes widened, and so did his smile.

Nobody noticed. They just carried on planning the wedding—the very-soon-to-take-place wedding—and the two of them played footsie and tried to keep a straight face.

Then her mother asked her to help clear the table and she had to scrabble for her shoes and came up desperately avoiding Mark's eye and trying not to laugh. She piled everything by the sink, poured the cream from the plastic carton into a big jug and set it on the table, and groaned with delight when she saw it was her mother's hot chocolate sauce pudding.

'This is the wickedest pudding in the world,' she warned Mark. 'In fact, you probably won't like it. I'd better have yours.'

'I'll risk it in the interests of your figure,' he said drily, and proceeded to risk it twice. 'Do you have any idea how much I miss home cooking?' he said to her mother with a sigh as he pushed away his plate. 'That was the best.'

'Thank you,' her mother said, beaming delightedly and going a delicate pink. 'You always were a plea-sure to feed.'

'He's good at washing up, as well. I thought he and Dad could do it and have a nice chat at the same time.'

However Dr Baker glanced at his watch regretfully and stood up. 'I'm going to have to love you and leave you, I'm afraid. I've got a patient who needs me—I should have been there earlier, really.'

'The lengths you'll go to to get out of the washing up,' Allie teased, but she was disappointed for Mark, because it meant there was no chance for him to talk to her father about general practice—and that was a disappointment for her, because she was desperately hoping he'd talk Mark out of it.

He made his farewells, and she heard him inviting Mark over during the week 'so we can have a good long chat about it'.

Good, she thought. Perhaps that will be enough.

'Why did he have to go?' she asked her mother quietly.

'It's Mr Sykes from the post office. He's very poorly. He's come home from the hospice, and your father doesn't think he'll last the night. He went down to see him first thing this morning before any of you were up.'

And her father, being the sort of man he was, would go and be with him now even though he wasn't on duty and there was another doctor paid to do the job. As if he wasn't busy enough already, she thought, not to mention exhausted.

She washed up with Mark, instead, after Daniel and Rosie had left, and her mother cleared up the kitchen and chatted to him about what he'd done in the last five years, and then much later, when they'd had a cup of tea and talked about the cottage, Mark looked at his watch and then at Allie.

'Do you have any plans for this evening?' he asked.

She shook her head. 'No. I'll stay here with Mum for a while and then come back later.'

'I can't talk you into a drink at the pub in Pulham on the way home?'

'With all your new friends? I might get sucked into the panto.'

He grinned. 'You might at that. They're short of beautiful young women. They asked about you the other day.'

'Did they?' she said with a laugh. 'Tell them I'm a ham. Tell them I've got a memory disorder that prevents me from learning lines. Tell them anything, but don't tell them I'm available, because I'm not!'

He smiled and shook his head. 'Was that a yes or a no to the drink?' he asked.

She hauled herself to her feet. 'Go on, then—but if you dump me in it with the panto I'll never speak to you again!'

'It's almost worth it,' Mark said softly to her mother, and her mother laughed.

'You don't mean that really.'

'No, I don't,' he agreed, and his eyes were warm and full of something she didn't dare analyse.

They went out to the drive, and when Mark pulled away with Allie right behind him, her mother paused beside her car door and looked down at her and said, 'I always did think he was right for you. I'm glad you've met up again.'

How perceptive of her, Allie thought, and with a wave she pulled off the drive, caught up with Mark who was waiting for her and followed him back to Pulham.

'This is silly, it means neither of us can drink.'

'We don't need to drink,' he said, and he was right,

of course. They didn't. They were both capable of enjoying themselves without the benefit of alcohol, and even if they hadn't been, the regulars would have seen to it. They recognised him, of course, after the panto meeting, and soon they were drawn into a fairly rowdy group.

It was a lively evening, and they ended playing darts—badly—and pool—slightly less badly—and leaving when the pub shut at ten-thirty that night.

He walked her to her car, and she wound down the window and he propped his hands on the door and leant in.

'Can I talk you into coffee?' he asked, and she could tell from the look in his eye that coffee was the last thing on his mind.

That was fine. It was the last thing on hers, too.

'Thanks. That would be nice. I'll park at home and come over.'

'I'll come and get you,' he told her, and brushed her lips with his.

Just lightly. Just enough to give her something other than driving to think about as she headed back to Audley.

She pulled up outside her house, shut off the engine and then jumped as the door swung open.

'You scared me to death,' she chided, laughing, and he pulled her out into his arms and kissed her, then reluctantly eased away.

'Come on. Let's go and find some mugs and make that coffee.'

They didn't bother. They went into his room, he drew her into his arms and she stayed here, locked in a gentle, undemanding and yet incredibly frustrating embrace until they both ran out of breath. Then he perched on the edge of the chest of drawers, pulled her into the vee of his legs and buried his face between her breasts.

She threaded her hands through his silky hair and sighed. She could feel the heat of his breath against her skin, and her legs felt weak and rubbery. His hands slid under the edge of her jumper and lifted it, and he dragged his tongue roughly across the lace of her bra, teasing the nipple with little sucking bites.

She arched against him, and with a groan he slipped the catch at the front and caught her aching, swollen breasts as they spilled into his waiting hands. He muttered something unintelligible, burying his face in their softness and rasping his beard gently against the tender skin.

She cried out, a tiny sound that made him rock against her, pulling her tighter against him. She could feel the solid pressure of his body against hers, the hard ridge of his arousal. Her legs threatened to buckle, and he moved, threading one leg between hers to support her. It just forced them closer together, and she clung to him and bit her lip as he suckled her breasts with a fierce tenderness that made her want to weep.

'This is driving me crazy,' he muttered a few moments later, lifting his head and locking her gaze with eyes like blazing coals. 'Stay with me, Allie,' he said gruffly. 'Let me make love to you.'

Something elemental shivered through her. She could stay. She could abandon her principles, dump the dubious asset of her virginity and give herself to him.

Or she could go, and look at herself in the mirror in the morning, because their relationship was going nowhere and it wasn't fair to play with his feelings in this way—or hers, come to that.

'I have to work in just seven hours,' she said quietly, struggling for common sense.

He sighed, laid a tender kiss on each oversensitive breast and fastened her bra for her, pulling her jumper down and straightening it.

'I'll walk you home—and don't argue,' he said tersely.

He was angry with her. She wanted to cry, because there was nothing she wanted more than to stay with him, but she knew it was a mistake.

He walked her to her door in silence, then without a word he pulled her into his arms and kissed her with almost savage gentleness. Then abruptly he pulled away. 'Goodnight, Allie. Thanks for today,' he said gruffly, and turning on his heel, he walked off and left her there.

She wanted to run after him, to stop him, to tell him she'd go back with him and make love with him after all, but she didn't. He was angry, and she wasn't quite sure why, and so she stayed there and watched him stride down the road as if the tarmac was blazing.

Then he was gone, turned the corner and out of sight, and she let herself in and went up to her lonely bed, and ached for him.

Regret kept her awake most of the night.

CHAPTER SEVEN

MONDAY was one of those days. Allie didn't have time to draw breath, but that was good. After Mark's abrupt manner the night before, she wasn't sure if she wanted time to think. She knew he was mad about the outcome of their evening, but whether he was mad with her, himself or just generally she didn't know.

It didn't matter, because there literally wasn't time to worry about it. They had to work together on patients, but there wasn't time to talk and they just had to get on with it. That was good. She didn't want time to talk until they had *enough* time, and they never would during the day, that was for sure.

Darren Forsey came back, his abscess much better now, to have his colostomy reversed. They put him back in the room he'd been in, and he settled immediately.

'He seems well,' Allie said to Anna in passing, and she nodded.

'Much better. Let's hope the op goes all right.'

Yes, Allie thought, it wouldn't do to take it for granted. It was too easy to expect everything to go right these days, but it didn't always.

For one family, though, things seemed to go right all at once. Claudia Hall had her long line out with a sigh of relief and went home, at the same time as her mum Jayne and baby Kieran. Their photos had been in the paper on Saturday, the football team had won their match, Claudia was better, the baby was alive and well, Jayne had got over her fall—what more could they have asked for? Happy endings all round, Allie thought with a smile.

'I'll miss her,' Allie said to Anna, watching the family leave the ward just before lunchtime. 'She's such a composed and courageous little girl.'

'So many of them are,' Anna said thoughtfully. 'It's one of the most humbling things about this job. I don't know where they find the strength some-times—or their parents, come to that. Watching your child suffer or maybe even die must be the most soul-destroying thing you could ever have to do, and yet so many of them do it with such acceptance and un-derstanding. I think I'd scream the place down.'

'Me, too,' Allie murmured. Just imagining losing Mark's baby was enough to devastate her. Not that there *was* one, or ever would be, but the thought—well, that was bad enough.

She never bothered to question the fact that it would be his child. Who else's? There was no one. Never had been, never would be. At least, no one that made her feel like that.

She blinked hard to clear her vision, and went to strip Claudia's bed and remake it. They had children coming in for operation the next day, others up in Theatre now who were coming back down, emergen-cies would come in—there was no time to stand around with unmade beds, because there was no tell-ing when they would be needed.

Anna fell into step beside her, automatically work-ing as a team as they remade the bed in seconds.

'Are you OK?' Anna asked as they worked, and Allie flashed her a bright smile.

'Fine. Just thinking about children and their parents. It gets to me sometimes.'

'Me too. I keep wishing I was married and had children, and then something happens and I'm really glad I'm not in that position and don't have to run the risk of going through it.' She straightened the cover and looked across the bed at Allie. 'How are you getting on with Mark, by the way? He's looking a little frayed round the edges this morning—have you two had a row?'

Allie thought of that kiss last night in his room. Well, more than a kiss, really, but not much. Just enough to wreck her sleep.

'No,' she said truthfully. 'No row. I expect he's just tired.'

Anna arched a speculative brow, and Allie shook her head. 'No,' she said firmly. 'I haven't worn him out.'

The phone rang, and Anna stifled what was obviously going to be a smart reply and went to answer it, leaving Allie to finish sorting out the bed. Anna came back to her just as she finished. 'That was Mark. He's down in Andrew's clinic. They're admitting a boy of twelve with aches and pains, general malaise and complete physical exhaustion. Andrew reckons he's got ME.'

'Oh, no,' Allie said with a groan. 'Poor lad. How long's he been like it?'

Anna shrugged. 'He didn't say. He's being admitted today for observation, and he's to have as quiet a room as possible. What can we shuffle round?'

'How about Darren?'

Anna nodded. 'I was thinking that. He's much better now, and he could really come out into the ward.

I know we said he could have his old room back, but
he doesn't really need it—not like this lad.'

'I'll tell him—he can come here, we'll swap the
beds round,' Allie said. She went into Darren's room
and found him watching television, lying on his bed
looking bright and lively.

'Darren, can we ask you a big favour?' she said.

He dragged his attention away from the television
screen and looked at her briefly. 'What's that?' he
asked.

'Could we move you out into the ward, so a very
sick boy can come in here and have absolute peace
and quiet? He's very ill, and he needs rest.'

Darren opened his mouth to argue, Allie thought,
and then shut it and shrugged. 'Sure. Where do you
want me to go?'

'Where Claudia was? I'll move the locker and bed,
so you don't have to worry about packing stuff up. If
you just hang on, I'll move you now.'

She knocked the brakes off the bed, pulled the
doors open to their locked position and pushed the
bed out into the ward. Then she swapped the two
beds, took the freshly made one into the single room
and brought the locker out, swapping them over as
well.

'OK? All settled? I know it means you can only
have your television on if you aren't disturbing anyone, but I'm sure this boy will be very grateful.'

Darren shrugged. ''S OK,' he said gruffly, and
looked around. 'Can I go down to the playroom and
see if there's anyone there I know?'

'Sure,' she agreed, and finished securing his bed
and the bed in the little room. Once everything was
tidy and ready, the clipboard hanging on the end of

the bed complete with empty charts, the glass and water jug on the locker, she went into the kitchen to get herself a drink and heard the door close softly behind her.

'Allie?'

She turned and met his eyes, and thought that Anna was right, he did look frayed around the edges. She gave him a cautious smile. 'Hi.'

He didn't smile back. He just looked at her for an age, then sighed. 'I'm sorry about last night,' he murmured. 'I was foul and crabby and I shouldn't have taken it out on you. I was just...'

'Frustrated?' she suggested, and he gave a cock-eyed grin that tipped her heart out of sync.

'Basically. I'm sorry.'

She felt herself melting inside, and smiled. 'Don't be. I felt the same.'

'I'm on call tonight,' he said tiredly. 'I feel bushed—I hardly slept a wink last night thinking about you.' He gave her a wry smile. 'I still want to be with you. How about a takeaway? We could eat it in my room and if I get called out, so be it.'

'And if you don't?' she asked gently.

His chuckle was sexy and knocked her off true again. 'That's a leading question.'

'I think the canteen might be safer,' she said with an answering smile.

He sighed and pulled her into his arms, hugging her gently. 'You're probably right. Six o'clock?'

'Sounds good. I must get on, we've got post-ops coming down from Recovery in a minute and they'll need me, and there's Andrew's ME case coming up from clinic. If I get out of here intact today it'll be a miracle.'

'Tell me about it,' he muttered, and with another hug he left her and went to find out who was bleeping him.

She would have been quite safe in his room—safe and alone. He was called away from the canteen to A&E, and no sooner had he come back than he was called up to the ward to see Nick Cottle, the boy with ME who was crying and restless and needed pain relief. It was a good job ME was accepted shorthand, he thought, he was much too tired to struggle with myalgic encephalomyelitis. He was too tired to struggle with anything much.

Not as tired as Nick, though. The boy was suffering from muscular aches and pains, flu-like symptoms but without the fever. They were going to run a whole battery of tests on him and expected to find nothing except a raised leucocyte count indicating that he'd been fighting an infection.

They might find something else, but Mark thought it unlikely. He'd had a friend with ME at school, and he'd been every bit as poorly as this boy and they'd never found a thing they could put their finger on, in three years.

Nick was tired, he was frustrated and he was sick of feeling ill. Mark could understand that. He was young and fit and liked sport. Now, suddenly, he could literally hardly walk, barely able to drag himself around.

'The last consultant I saw told me it was psychological and I should go into a rehabilitation unit, but there was a programme about it on the television and I knew straight away it wasn't right for me. I'm not making it up, I promise,' he told Mark with the last of his strength.

Mark believed him. His friend had been a keen sportsman and had been devastated by the loss of his fitness, and the only reason he'd been depressed had been because the disability depressed him. It certainly wasn't the other way around, as some people tried to imply.

He upped the pain relief, chatted to the boy for a while and watched as he drifted back off to sleep. Good. He didn't need to be here, he needed to be at home with his parents in the care of an understanding GP.

Not in hospital, in the care of a houseman who wouldn't be involved in his follow-up. Mark sighed heavily with impatience. He was finding the wait until he was able to start in general practice irksome and frustrating. This wasn't what he was cut out for, and although he loved the children and did the job to the best of his ability, it wasn't enough to make him happy.

Allie, now—Allie could make him happy, he thought tiredly, if he only had the strength to take advantage of her. He trudged back from the ward to the canteen, and found her curled up in the corner with a cup in her hand, asleep.

Poor girl, she didn't look as if she'd slept any better than he had last night. He took the cup out of her nerveless fingers, woke her gently and walked her home.

'I'm not going to get any peace tonight, I can tell,' he said as he turned her into his arms. 'You go and catch up with your sleep, you look shattered.'

'At least I can go to bed,' she said softly, her warm, gentle palm cradling his cheek. 'You have to stay up.'

'I can go to bed,' he told her with a wry grin. 'I just have to sleep in my clothes. That's fine. I've done it before. No doubt I'll do it again.' He turned his head into her hand and kissed her palm tenderly. 'Don't worry about me.'

'I'm not worried, I'm just feeling sorry for you. Do you want to come in for coffee?' she added, and his bleep sounded in his pocket, answering her question.

He shook his head, conjuring up a wry, regretful smile. 'I'll see you tomorrow. Sleep tight.' He kissed her, a frustratingly innocent kiss that left him aching for more, and went back to the hospital.

Monday seemed to set the tone for the week, Allie thought. They were endlessly busy, but not with anything demanding, just a continual flow of children with flu and gastric upsets and so forth.

That worried Allie, because young Nick Cottle who was suffering from ME was vulnerable to other infections and so they were trying to keep him as isolated as possible without actually barrier nursing him. He was exhausted, in constant pain and hardly able to do anything for himself, and an important part of every day for him was a good sound sleep during the afternoon.

That coincided with a rest period enforced for the sake of the younger children on the ward, and so the ward tended to be fairly quiet.

Noise didn't seem to worry him, though. He was so exhausted he slept anyway, although the night staff said he hadn't slept through the night.

Still, it wasn't for long. He was in to undergo tests

to make sure he didn't have any other underlying condition that had been overlooked, so he had to have endless blood samples taken, throat swabs, urine and faecal samples sent off for analysis—endless indignities and irritations.

'I'm sorry you've got to put up with all this,' Allie said gently, preparing to take yet another syringe full of blood for more tests on Wednesday morning.

'That's OK,' he murmured, watching her wearily as she worked. 'I haven't got anything else to do.'

She perched on the edge of the bed and smiled. 'No, I suppose not. It must be very frustrating to be so young and fit and healthy one minute and then not be able to do anything the next.' She tightened the cuff on his arm, slid the needle home and withdrew the blood while he watched. 'That's that one, now for the next,' she said, swapping syringes, and repeating the procedure. 'So, tell me how you went down with this mystery illness. Was it sudden?'

He nodded. 'Yeah. I had sort of flu—I just felt dreadful, and instead of getting better, I just couldn't seem to shake it off. I got a bit better, flu-wise, but I was so tired. It was like I'd been up all night for weeks, but I hadn't.'

'Ever felt like that before?'

He shook his head. 'Not that tired, no. I don't usually get tired. Then Mum started to get worried when I couldn't get up after about two weeks and I was still spending all my time in bed.'

'She must have been very concerned,' Allie said thoughtfully.

'She was. The doctor thought I was just skiving, but Mum knows me better than that. Anyway, then I got a bit better, and the next thing was I'd gone back to school and they had to come and fetch me because I couldn't move. I'd done football and I was so tired I literally couldn't walk. I just lay on the pitch and they had to carry me in.'

'Good heavens.' She released the band on his arm, withdrew the needle and pressed down on the puncture wound, holding it for him for a minute to prevent it leaking and bruising him. 'So when was this?'

'Last spring. I spent most of the summer term off, and then when I still couldn't do anything the doctor said I needed to see a psychiatrist, because there was nothing wrong with me—he'd done all these tests and didn't find anything, just like you're doing. Anyway, he said I was just attention-seeking and I had depression and needed a shrink.'

Allie looked at his face, the hollows under his eyes, the exhaustion evident in his expression, and smiled understandingly. 'And what do you think?' she asked, fixing a plaster over the needle hole in his arm. 'Do you need a shrink?'

He laughed without humour. 'No, of course I don't. I'm just ill. I hurt, my hands and feet get pins and needles all the time, I can't concentrate, I'm so tired I can't stand, I can hardly walk any more and nobody believes me—' He broke off, his eyes filling, and Allie hugged him and held him while he cried.

'It's OK, Nick. We believe you. Don't upset yourself,' she murmured, rocking him gently against her shoulder. 'Let's get these tests off and make sure there's nothing else wrong that nobody's picked up, and then we can go from there, but please believe me, nobody here thinks you're making it up and we all want to find out what's wrong with you.'

He sniffed and scrubbed his nose on his sleeve, and

Allie found him a box of tissues in his locker and ruffled his hair affectionately. 'OK now?'

He nodded and lay back against the pillows looking wretched. 'I'm so tired—even talking makes me tired,' he said wearily.

'Have a sleep. I'll shut your blinds.'

Allie tipped the blinds down so the light was diffused, collected up all her bits and pieces onto the trolley and left him to rest.

She saw Mark later and told him what Nick had said, and he nodded. 'He told me the same. I'm sure it's ME. I've seen it before. Don't worry, I believe the kid, and Andrew does as well. Did you send the tests off for analysis?'

She nodded. 'They all went off this morning. I just feel so sorry for him because nobody will take it seriously.'

'We will,' he assured her. 'Andrew says he's more and more convinced it's physical and that we'll find a cure soon, but until then we just have to play it by ear. His parents are talking about taking him to a homeopath or herbalist—I have to say it won't hurt, and who knows, it might help. Apparently we can't do anything—they might as well have a go.'

Allie blinked. 'You believe in homeopathic remedies?'

'I don't know. I'm open to suggestion. In the meantime we need to get the results of these tests.'

They all came back negative. Nothing untoward, except a slightly raised white cell count to indicate he'd been fighting an infection, which was exactly what they'd expected.

Mark was monitoring him daily, and by the end of the week Andrew Barrett came up to see him again,

compared the results of Mark's observations with his
ward record and test results, and sent him home. They
could do nothing for him, and the ward routine was
too noisy and busy for him and was making him more
tired.

'Poor kid,' Mark said quietly, watching him go. 'I
wonder what he's going to be like in the future?'

'Who knows?' Allie murmured.

'Not us, that's for sure. Doesn't it frustrate you that
you won't know?'

She thought of the thousands of children who
passed through the ward each year, and smiled ruefully. 'No. I do what I can. I make sure that any
treatment they have is as untraumatic as possible, that
I've been as kind and as understanding with them and
their parents as I can be, that nothing is left undone
that could have helped them, that they aren't lonely
or afraid if I can avoid it—that's why I'm here, what
I do, what I'm about.'

'And then they go home and you don't have any
idea how they get on.'

'But the vast majority are fine—they go home fit
and well, because we've done our job, and they don't
need us any more. So, no, it doesn't frustrate me—
well, not often. And anyway, we do have follow-up
when it's necessary,' she added. 'We have loads of
kids who come to us over and over again—kids like
Claudia.'

He was still watching the doorway, though Nick
and his parents were long out of sight, and he gave a
sigh that seemed to come from the depths of his soul.
'I saw your father last night,' he said out of the blue.

'How is he?'

'Fine. We had a long chat. He's a nice guy.'

'I love him to bits, but he's my father. I'm biased. Any news about the cottage?'

A smile flashed across his face, lighting his eyes and driving away the shadows. 'Yes. I have to ring after twelve to see if the sale's completed. If it is, I'm going to sneak out at lunchtime and pick up the key from the agent. I won't have time to go over there until tonight, though, but I thought I'd have a look then—make sure I still like it! Are you game?'

'Absolutely,' she assured him with a smile. 'I can't wait to see it again—I expect it will look awful without all her knick-knacks and bits and pieces—empty and grim and in serious need of redecoration, I imagine, but at least you'll be able to really look at it properly and crawl all over it, and I'm sure you'll still like it. You couldn't fail.'

'You have such faith,' he said mournfully. 'I hope you're right.'

'Of course I'm right,' she said with more confidence than she felt. 'Is the electricity on?'

'Should be, and the phone. What time do you finish?'

'Three today.'

He gave a short huff of laughter. 'Lucky you. I'll be here till six at least, I think. We've got a clinic. Look, I'll catch you later. We can have supper in the pub, if you like. I don't know what the kitchen will be like, and there's nothing to sit on. What are you doing this weekend?'

'Furniture-shopping?' she suggested, and he laughed.

'Pencil it in. If it needs too much decorating I might not bother yet. We'll see. I'll ring you once I know it's mine.'

'Do that.'

He looked round, saw Anna and winked. 'Consider yourself kissed,' he said with a smile, and walked away, leaving her with a sappy smile on her face and no hope of hiding it from her eagle-eyed superior.

Anna walked up beside her and looked her up and down. 'You seem very pleased with yourself,' she said without hesitation. 'How's the great romance?'

'Anna, you do exaggerate, there's no great romance,' she flannelled, trying to put her off. 'He's getting the cottage today. We're going out to look at it. That's all.'

'Fun. I love house-hunting and moving and things. Are you going to live with him?'

Allie looked at her in amazement. 'Me?' she asked, stunned.

'What's so odd about that? Anyone would think I'd asked you if you were going to move in with the Marquis de Sade, for heaven's sake. He's not that bad, surely?'

Allie shook her head. 'No, of course not, but we don't have that sort of a relationship.'

Anna stared at her as if she was crazy. 'You don't? What a waste,' she said bluntly. 'Right, I'm going for coffee. Can you have a look at Tanya's drip, please? I think it needs moving. Oh, and Stores rang. They're short of catheters, can we avoid using them if possible until later today or tomorrow? I said we'd make the kids wet themselves instead. You might want to con- ciliate if they ring back.'

'Cheers! You're a star, Anna. You go for coffee now and leave me clearing up your mess.'

Anna laughed and tossed her the keys and walked calmly off the ward, leaving Allie in charge.

                    *   *   *

The doorbell rang at a little before seven, and Allie opened it to find Mark there, dressed in jeans and a thick sweater, keys dangling from his fingertips.

'Got it,' he said with a grin. 'I'm now the proud owner of Church Cottage.'

'Wonderful!' she said with a laugh. 'Are we going now?'

'Soon as you're ready.'

'I'm ready. I'll just grab my jacket.'

She hooked it off the banisters, yelled goodbye to Lucy and Beth, and followed him down the path, still shrugging her arms into the coat. The Friday night traffic was busy, but he wove through it and drove the few miles out to Pulham without any trouble, pulling up outside the dark little cottage just before seven-thirty.

'All we have to do now is find our way in and switch on the lights—I hope they haven't turned the electricity off at the mains, because of course I forgot to bring a torch!'

'Of course,' Allie agreed. 'I've got a pen-torch on my keyring, if that's any good to you.'

'Hopefully we won't need it,' he said, opening the front gate and walking up the dark path towards the front door.

Suddenly the garden was flooded with light, and he threw her a grin. 'Good. The power's still on and the sensor lights are working. That's a comfort.'

He slipped the key in the lock, turned it and went in, flicking on the light. Allie followed him, watching his face as he looked around. It was only when he let his breath out on a sigh of relief that she realised she'd been holding hers.

'Thank God for that—I *do* like it,' he said with a laugh.

'I said you would.'

'Right—first things first. I've got a kettle and some coffee and milk, two mugs and a spoon. Let's go and investigate the kitchen.'

It was much as before—spotlessly clean now, because clearly someone had been in and scoured the whole place from top to toe, but still in need of re-fitting and redecorating. The bathroom was better, more recently painted, and the old-fashioned suite with the roll-top bath and high-level cistern over the loo was at least in keeping with the cottage.

They left the kettle fizzing gently and went upstairs in some trepidation to investigate the bed. 'Oh, wow,' Allie said softly, seeing it properly for the first time. It had heavily carved, solid mahogany ends, with short turned posts sticking up from each corner and the most wonderful patina of old age.

'How did we miss it?' she asked, stunned.

'It was covered in blankets to protect it, Gerald said, so the carving didn't get full of dust. He told me the cleaner had polished it.'

'It is beautiful,' Allie murmured in awe, stroking her fingers over the smooth, inches-deep gloss on the top of the footboard. 'I can imagine it with a feather mattress, all soft and cosy and inviting.'

'Wonderful—especially for allergy sufferers,' he said drily.

'You've got no soul,' she complained, giving the wood one last, lingering stroke.

'Terrible roll-together, feather mattresses. That's why people used to have so many children.'

'They had so many children because there was no

television to keep them occupied and there was nothing else to do in the evenings,' Allie retorted with a
smile. 'Now we're all stuck in front of soap operas
and motoring programmes.'

'Is that good or bad?'

She laughed. 'I don't know. Search me.'

'Is that an invitation?'

Her breath jammed in her throat, and she laughed
and turned away, heading for the stairs. 'You should
be so lucky.'

'I should. It's about time my luck changed. What
do you think of the oak boards? Aren't they lovely?
I think I might just have rugs on them and not bother
with carpets. It seems a shame to cover them.'

She stopped on the stairs and looked at the floor of
the landing, just below her eye level. There was a
deep, rich shine to the wood that only hundreds of
years of love could have achieved.

'You can't cover them,' she agreed, glad of the
change of subject. It was getting all a little too hot
for comfort!

She went back to the kitchen and made them coffee, and they sat on the hearth and looked at the
beams and the funny little nooks and crannies in the
huge chimney breast, and he put his arm around her
shoulders and drew her in to his side and hugged her.

'It's lovely, isn't it?' he said. 'It wasn't a mistake.'

'No, it wasn't a mistake,' she assured him, trying
to concentrate on the cottage and not on the firm, hard
length of his thigh pressed against her side, the feel
of his hand on her shoulder, the slow rise and fall of
his chest under the soft, thick sweater that felt so good
to touch.

She could easily be lulled by him into something foolish, something wonderful and warm and altogether too precious.

That *would* be a mistake.

CHAPTER EIGHT

THEY shopped for furniture the next day. Allie wasn't on duty on Sunday morning, and she had the whole of that Saturday free as well. Mark unrepentantly stole all of it to drag her round the junk shops looking for suitable bits and pieces, and by lunchtime on Saturday they'd acquired a vanload of furniture scattered all around the town.

Mark had anything he wanted put on one side, and then he hired a van for the afternoon and they went round collecting it all up and carting it back to the cottage.

While he took the van back, she set about with first vinegar and then beeswax, cleaning and polishing the wood until it gleamed. By the time he came back the table and chairs were done, and she was halfway through a chest of drawers that was destined for his bedroom—if they could get it up the stairs.

'Wow,' he said admiringly, standing back to study her handiwork. 'They look better—thanks.' He glanced at the half-done chest, and pulled a face. 'I wonder—before you put too much effort in on that chest, don't you think we ought to see if it'll fit?'

She sat back on her heels, looked from him to the narrow little stairwell and laughed. 'I don't think there's the slightest danger that it will go up that tiny little crack in the floorboards, but we can try.'

They pulled the drawers out, she took the front end and he took the back, and they sweated and juggled and swore and squashed their fingers, trying it from all angles, and then suddenly it seemed to sort itself out and it was through the gap, up onto the landing and safely ensconced in the bedroom.

'I'm amazed.'

Allie laughed. 'Not as amazed as me. I've been studying it for the past half-hour trying to work out how it would fit!'

He sat on the edge of the bed, perched on the iron frame that cried out for a mattress, and pulled her onto his lap. 'Thanks. You're a love.'

'My pleasure.' She peered over his shoulder at the iron springs in the bedframe. 'You need a mattress,' she said, and he nodded.

'I do. Let's go and choose one. The shops are still open—well, the big furniture superstores are. We can go and try them all out.'

Allie looked at herself and laughed at him. 'I'm a mess—I'm covered in beeswax.'

'Wash. It comes off. Your clothes look fine, and anyway, nobody's going to look at you.'

'They will if I leave a nasty streak of beeswax on a new mattress,' she assured him drily. 'And anyway, you don't need my help.'

'Yeah, I do. You'll be fine. Come on, I can't wait to move in and I can't sleep on the springs.'

She gave them another look and had to agree. They looked wickedly uncomfortable. 'Do you think you'd do better to buy a divan and rest it on the top? I know someone who's done that—they screwed blocks to the bottom of the divan base to stop it sliding around, and it's a super bed. It's high, but it's rather fun and it looks the part somehow, and it has to be more comfortable than those springs!'

He laughed and stood up, depositing her on her feet. 'You could be right. Come on—let's measure it and go shopping.'

'I like the look of this one—here, lie down and try it out.'

'Oh, but I don't think—'

'Oh, madam, it's most important it suits both of you,' the salesman chipped in. 'Please don't feel embarrassed—everybody tries out the beds.'

She opened her mouth to argue, but Mark didn't give her a chance.

'Quite—it has to suit us both,' he insisted, a devil dancing in his eyes. 'Come on, try it.'

She looked dubiously at the bed, and at Mark stretched out full length on his back, arms folded behind his head, an expectant expression on his face, and weighed the futility of arguing against the embarrassment of explaining. Defeated either way, she gingerly lowered herself down onto the mattress.

'That's it,' the salesman said. 'You two just make yourselves comfortable for a minute. I'll come back to you later—feel free to try out any of the other beds, and try all sorts of different positions, as well. You won't always want to lie on your back.'

Mark made a strangled noise, and Allie shot him a warning glance. He rolled to face her, barely stifling a laugh, and grinned wickedly. 'My old flatmate's got a very interesting book—it's got all sorts of positions in it,' he murmured, and she felt a hot tide of colour rush over her face.

'Shh!' she whispered, a giggle rising up to choke her. 'You are incorrigible.'

'Nonsense. It's your mind. Besides, I need to know

if we're going to roll together and make hundreds of babies.'

'Not a chance,' she said emphatically, swinging her legs over the side of the bed. 'Anyway, it's too soft.'

'How about that one there? It's got a rigid base.'

He led her across the showroom to another bed, and lying down without a trace of self-consciousness, he patted the mattress beside him.

'Won't you lie down beside me? said the spider to the fly,' he murmured.

'I think you've got that wrong,' she told him, swinging her legs up onto the bed and lying down. A sigh of delight escaped her, and she looked at him. 'Bliss. This one's really comfortable.'

'Lie on your side and face me.'

'Is this a trick?' she asked warily, and he laughed and shook his head.

'No trick. You've got lush curves—it may not support your waist.'

'Why does it matter?' she asked. 'It's your bed.'

He reached for her, cupping her cheek with his hand. 'You really want to go into this here?'

Her heart started to pound suddenly, her chest rising and falling much faster all of a sudden. He noticed, his eyes narrowing, and he leant forwards and kissed her, just very briefly. 'Is it all right on your side?' he asked.

She nodded, speechless and unable to drag her eyes from his. They were like pebbles in a stream, dark and light mingled together, changing, shifting, and she couldn't work out what he was telling her.

She had the distinct feeling she didn't want to know—not right there in the shop, with the salesman from hell bearing down on them at a rate of knots.

'How are you getting on?' he boomed heartily.

'Fine. I'll take one of these. When can we have it delivered?' Mark asked, swinging his legs over the side and getting to his feet in one easy movement. Allie stood up more slowly, gathering her thoughts and feelings as she did so.

Their relationship was moving on like wildfire, and she really ought to put the brakes on. It wasn't fair to either of them to keep on doing this, but nothing had been said that made her think he was serious. It could be that he was just having fun.

More than likely. He was twenty-seven—if he was the marrying kind, he would have done it by now.

She smiled absently at the salesman, retrieved her handbag and coat from the floor and followed Mark to the desk to deal with the paperwork.

'It's in stock—we could deliver tomorrow morning,' he said, consulting a list, and Mark nodded.

'That would be good. I'm at work all week.'

'Most people are—that's why we offer the week-end delivery service. Sign here—thank you, sir. It'll be with you in the morning, any time after nine o'clock. I hope you both find it very comfortable and spend many happy hours in it.'

Mark mumbled something unintelligible, Allie gave him what she thought might be a smile but was probably just a hideous rictus, and they made it through the door just before Mark's laughter bubbled up.

'You should have told him!' Allie protested. 'You deliberately let him think I was your wife or your girlfriend or something.'

'You *are* my girlfriend,' he argued, and then looked thoughtful. 'Aren't you?'

She shrugged. 'I suppose so. Depends how you define it. That salesman obviously thought we were something rather more than we are.'

He looked at her over the top of the car, arms folded on the roof, eyes unreadable in the poor lighting of the car park. 'You could have told him yourself,' he pointed out.

He was right. She could have done, but she hadn't really known how to, and it hadn't really mattered.

No, what was puzzling her was Mark's insistence that she should try the bed, almost as if it mattered.

Why?

They left the car park, Allie still confused, and bought fish and chips and headed back to the cottage. It was still early, only eight o'clock, and they finished polishing the chest of drawers and put it all back together, then stood back and admired it.

'Excellent,' he said contentedly. 'Thanks, Allie. I owe you.'

'Good. I'll collect. I want a hot bath, a cup of tea and bed in that order, starting shortly.'

He gave a wry grin. 'No bed and not enough hot water for a bath, I'm afraid. I can make you a cup of tea?'

She shook her head. 'I'm bushed. I have to work tomorrow at twelve, and I have to blitz the house. I really wouldn't mind an early night.'

So he took her back, and in the morning she had a lie-in and then cleaned her room and attacked the bathroom and kitchen before going to work.

It was odd without Mark. He was there most of the time, and when she worked the weekend and he didn't, it seemed quite strange. Empty, almost, despite the bustle, not that Sundays were usually that busy.

It was an odd sort of busyness, a disordered, chaotic sort of mishmash of patients most of whom had come via A&E.

There were always more accidents over the weekend, and GP admissions tended to pick up. Perhaps it was because parents who were at work all week had time to notice their children at the weekend, or perhaps it was just to do with the extra activities and different routines, but nearly always there was a little rush of emergencies.

At least without the routine admissions for surgery and investigations they had more time to deal with them, and they discharged as many children on Friday as possible to get them home with their families over the weekend. It helped with staffing, and it helped the children.

And it made room for the weekend rush of sports injuries and household accidents, of which there were always several.

And then there were the other ones, the cases that didn't fit the mould.

Boys like the one admitted that Sunday shortly after Allie arrived on the ward. He'd been found in the park, the victim of a beating, with no ID on him and unable to remember his name. He looked about fourteen or fifteen, so he was admitted to Paediatrics for rest and observation. The police had been called to the hospital, and had followed him up to the ward hoping he would regain his memory.

'We need to know who he is—his parents will be worried sick,' the policeman told Allie. Dave was a family man, a genuinely nice person who cared about the people he met through his work. Allie had seen him on more than one occasion, and she'd grown to respect and trust him.

Their young victim, however, was not so trusting. 'I don't know who I am,' he said in a Scots accent. 'I've no idea. I just woke up with a headache and found I was lying in the park.'

'You can't remember how you got there?' the policeman asked him.

He shook his head, very cautiously, and winced. 'No. Sorry.'

But he looked wary and unhappy, and after a while Allie stopped Dave and asked him to wait outside. 'He needs to rest,' she explained, and ushered him out. 'Ask Pearl—she'll make you a cup of tea if you're nice to her.'

'I'm always nice to Pearl,' he said with a smile, and she left them together and went back to the boy, closing the door behind her.

'Are you all right?' she asked softly after a moment.

'Yeah.' He looked sullen and wary and unwilling to talk, but she persisted, talking about his injuries and telling him what they were going to do about them. All the time she looked around, sometimes at him, sometimes busying herself with other things, always keeping a surreptitious eye on him without him being aware of it.

He definitely looked uneasy, she thought, and at times on the verge of tears.

She paused, giving up her busywork with the charts for a moment. 'I just wondered—the people that attacked you. Are they likely to come looking for you?'

He was silent for a long while, then he shook his

head. 'No. I mean, I don't remember, but I don't think
so,' he added warily.

'Did you know them?'

Again, he shook his head. 'Um—don't think so. I
said, I can't remember.'

Why didn't she believe him? Was it because his
eyes were sliding every which way but at her? Or
because his fingers were plucking the sheet ner-
vously? Or the chalk-white line around his mouth?

'What about your parents?' she asked carefully.
No, she wasn't wrong, there was a definite flicker of
fear in his eyes. Surely his parents hadn't done this?

'I don't know who they are. I don't know who I
am. I can't remember,' he repeated, and clammed up,
seeming to shrink into the pillows.

Allie hung the charts back on the end of the bed.
'OK. Don't worry, it'll come. I'll keep the policeman
out so you can rest, OK?'

'Is he still here?' he asked, and the fear was show-
ing in his voice now. Allie pretended not to notice.

'I'm afraid so. He's waiting for you to remember
something. It could be days, though, before your
memory comes back—do you want me to ask him to
go away, and we'll ring him if you remember anything?'

He relaxed visibly, his shoulders dropping inches.
What was going on? Allie thought. What would drive
him into hiding?

'That would be cool,' he said, his voice taut as if
he didn't quite believe it.

Allie slipped out and spoke to Dave. 'I don't think
there's any point you being here,' she told him. 'He's
obviously frightened, but he won't say who he is, and
he seems to be frightened of the police. Can I ask you

to leave him with us for a few days? I'll ring if he tells me anything I think you want to hear, and we'll keep an eye on him. Perhaps in the meantime you could look through pictures of missing kids or whatever, just in case.'

'I don't want him legging it,' he warned.

'He won't leg it. He can't stand at the moment and his ribs are cracked. I think you're safe for a few days.'

'Just make darned sure you don't lose him. I'll come back later. I'll go and look at mugshots.'

'I won't lose him.'

She watched the policeman go, and went back in. 'He's gone—just for a while. Do me a favour? My job's on the line here. Don't try anything, will you?'

He looked away. ''Course not.'

She perched a hip on the end of his bed and laid a comforting hand over his foot. 'They just want to get whoever did this to you, and they need to find out who you are so you can be returned to your parents.'

His foot seemed to flinch under her hand as she said the last word. Why?

'Can we make you up a name? Something you'd like to be called if you weren't called Jason or Hamish or whatever?'

He looked at her warily. 'Call me Jimmy,' he said.

'Is that your name?'

He shook his head. 'It's what you call Scotsmen, isn't it? Jimmy? That'll do. Anyway, I told you, I don't remember my name.'

'Of course not. OK, Jimmy. I'll leave you to sleep. Press the button on the end of this wire if you need anything, OK?'

She squeezed his foot gently and stood up.

'Nurse?'

'Uh-huh?'

'Thanks.'

She smiled at him. 'The name's Allie—and it's OK. Just don't take off.'

Another flicker of fear, and then he nodded and closed his eyes.

Poor kid. What on earth was going on with him? And what was a lad who sounded so Scottish doing down here in East Anglia? It should make it easier to trace him, but for the moment her gut instinct was to let him hole up and not tell the police too much. Maybe if she could find out who he was and why he was so frightened of his parents, it would help.

He slept all afternoon, and when she went in at five to check him again, he opened his eyes and looked at her.

'Hi, Jimmy.'

'Hi.'

'How are you?'

'Better, thanks. I think the painkillers might be working. It's nice to be warm.'

Warm? Her worst fears rose up and demanded recognition. His clothes had been far from clean; under the blood and grime of today's fight they'd been unwashed for ages. So had he. She'd washed him all over, checking for bruises and scrapes that needed attention, and he'd started to smell a little less pungent, but he needed a good bath. Perhaps tomorrow.

For now, she needed to work out why it was so novel to be warm, and there was only one answer.

He was a runaway.

'Jimmy, why are you hiding?' she asked softly, sitting beside him on the edge of the bed and taking his hand. 'What's frightened you so much you had to run away?'

His eyes slid wildly round the room. 'I don't know what you mean.'

'Don't play games. I'm not going to shop you to the police. Have you got problems at home?'

His eyes flooded with tears, and he blinked hard. 'No.'

'Because you're not there?'

Stubborn silence.

'Do they harm you, Jimmy? Is that why you're afraid?'

'I'm saying nothing.'

'Is it your father?'

'He's dead.'

Progress. 'Your stepfather?'

Bingo. As if the floodgates had opened, his misery poured out. 'He hits my mother. He rapes her. She lets him. He does it all the time. I tried to stop him, and he hit me and threw me down the stairs. I broke my leg.'

'I noticed it had been broken. Didn't you tell the police?'

'He said it was an accident. He said I was having a row with my mother and when I hit her he tried to stop me. He said he pushed me out of the room and I fell down the stairs. My mother backed him up. It was just a lie, but they believed him. They thought I was making trouble, trying to come between them. They sent me back, and he beat me unconscious. When I came round, I left.'

She took a deep breath to settle her revulsion. 'What about your leg?'

'My leg was still in plaster. I hid in Glasgow—we

lived there. The police found me and sent me back again. They didn't listen to me. He beat me again. My mum just stood there and watched him—she's supposed to be my mother, for God's sake, and she stood there and watched him pulverise me—'

His voice cracked, and Allie pulled him gently into her arms and cradled him while he sobbed his heart out.

She heard the door open and close behind her, and hoped it wasn't the policeman. It wasn't. It was another nurse, needing her for drugs.

'Jimmy, I'll be back,' she told him. 'I have to go and do something, then I'll come back and talk to you, OK?'

'Don't tell the police.'

The fear in his voice would have stopped her if nothing else had. 'I won't,' she promised.

It was an hour before she could get back to him, and then it was only briefly. The policeman came back and spoke to her, and she was evasive. 'He hasn't told me his name. He's not well yet. I'd rather you didn't talk to him.'

'Just a quick word.'

She went in with him, and Jimmy's eyes were full of mistrust. 'You promised,' he said accusingly to Allie.

'I couldn't make him stay away, Jimmy. He's got a job to do.'

'Jimmy?' Dave said enquiringly, shooting Allie a glance.

'It's what we've decided to call him for now. It's better than "Oi, you," we thought.'

Dave nodded. 'OK, Jimmy. Anything you want to tell me?'

'Have you been talking to him?' he asked Allie abruptly.

Dave didn't bat an eyelid. 'She's told me nothing, son. I just wondered if you wanted to.'

'No. Nothing to tell.'

'OK. Well, if you decide to talk to me, I'll be right outside. You don't want to give me your parents' phone number or address so we can contact them and tell them you're safe?'

'No. I told you, I can't remember anything.'

Dave nodded. 'OK. Well, like I said, I'll be outside if you change your mind.'

Dave went out, and Jimmy turned accusing eyes on Allie. 'What did you tell him?'

'Nothing. I promise. I asked him not to come in. He said he had to.'

'He suspects something.'

Allie sighed and sat down on the bed. 'Of course he does. You're brought in filthy, beaten up, with apparent memory loss, and you won't talk to the police. A normal kid in those circumstances would be begging the police to find out who he was and locate his parents. It's obvious there's something wrong. You don't have to be a rocket scientist to work it out, Jimmy, and we see a lot of this.'

He was silent for a long while, then he shifted in the bed and looked at her, then looked away again. 'Sorry.'

The apology was grudging, but Allie didn't mind. He trusted her again, and that meant she might be able to help him. 'It's all right. I'm going to get another doctor to look at you, if I can.'

'A shrink?'

'No. A paediatrician—a children's doctor. He can

make sure you're all right. How long have you been on the run, Jimmy?'

'A year, nearly.'

'Have you taken drugs?'

He shook his head. 'I'm not stupid.'

'How have you lived?'

He looked away. 'Scavenging from bins, stealing, that sort of thing. I find things in skips and sell them—I sold a table once for a hundred pounds to a junk shop.'

'What about sex?'

His eyes dropped. 'There was a man, once. Last summer. I was hungry. He said he'd feed me if I'd go home with him.' He was silent for ages, his face haunted. 'I learnt my lesson.'

She shook her head sadly. 'I'll get Mark to look at you—can I tell him this?'

'Why?'

'Because if he's going to give you the best care, he needs to know the truth, Jimmy.'

'Can you trust him?'

She didn't hesitate. 'Yes, absolutely. He's a good friend.'

Jimmy sighed and gave in. 'OK. But only him.'

'Right.'

She left the room, shrugged at Dave and went into the office to ring Mark in his room. He answered on the second ring.

'It's Allie. Can you do me a favour? Can you come up to the ward?'

'Sure. Give me five minutes.'

He was there in less than that, and she took him to one side and quickly filled him in. He was horrified and disgusted. 'Poor little blighter. Where is he?'

'In the single over there. Mark, be careful. He's very wary.'

'I'll be all right. Are you coming?'

'Do you want me to?'

'Initially. We'll see after that.'

She stayed just long enough for Jimmy to relax, and then she left them alone, went into the office and phoned the paediatric medical social worker, filling her in briefly. She wanted to come straight to the ward, but reluctantly agreed to see Jimmy the next day, while Allie was on duty.

After an age Mark emerged from Jimmy's room and found Allie in the office tackling the rota.

'How is he?' she asked.

'OK. He's pretty skinny and undernourished, but not too bad. There's no obvious sign of sexual assault at any time, and from what he said I don't think he's in any danger of having got HIV from this guy in Blackpool—he got away before anything too bad happened.'

'Thank goodness for that. What was he doing in Blackpool?'

Mark shrugged. 'Who knows? He's lived in Bristol, Edinburgh, Leeds, Blackpool, London, and now here. He's remarkably well, considering, but he's got slight congestion in one lung. I want him on antibiotics for that, I want a load of blood tests, a psychiatric assessment, anything else you can think of that will keep him in until he's stronger and fitter. And I want the police kept away from him as long as possible, because he's clearly distressed and with good reason.'

'So would you like to tell Dave that?' she said,

indicating the policeman sitting patiently outside the room.

'Sure.'

He went over to the policeman and had a long chat, then Dave stood up and went into the room, spoke briefly to Jimmy and left the ward.

'What did you say?'

'Told him we have to co-operate with each other, and at the moment his presence was upsetting the boy and hindering his recovery.'

'Has he gone?'

'He'll be back. Are you finished now?'

She realised it was almost nine. 'Um—yes. I have to hand over to the Night Sister. She'll be here in a minute—ah, there she is. Why?'

'Come and have a coffee.'

'OK.'

She told the Night Sister the bare minimum about Jimmy, filled her in on the rest of the ward and then left. Mark's door was opened, and she walked in, kicked the door shut behind her and went straight into his arms and howled.

'Shh, love, it's all right.'

'It's not fair,' she said after a few minutes when she'd hiccuped to a halt. 'You've got kids like Claudia with parents that do everything to make life as smooth as possible, loving parents who have the most awe-inspiring relationship with their daughter, and then you get a kid like Jimmy with a stepfather who tries to kill him and a mother who takes the man's side against her own son! How can she do that? And what about the others? Does he have any brothers or sisters?'

'There are no other children at home,' he assured her. 'They've all left. He's the youngest.'

'Thank God for small mercies.' She pushed out of his arms, went into the little shower room and grabbed a handful of loo paper, blew her nose hard and went back to him, plopping down onto the bed with a heavy sigh. 'Sorry, I'm not very good company.'

'That's all right, I don't need entertaining with bright and witty conversation all the time. That's what friends are for.'

She smiled up at him, immensely grateful for his understanding. 'Thanks. I need a hug.'

He sat beside her, drew her into his arms and kissed her firmly. 'There. Better?'

'Much.'

'Good.' He lay down and patted the mattress beside him. 'Come and have a cuddle.'

She couldn't resist it. She lay down in his arms, hard up against him, and sighed. 'This bed has terrible roll-together,' she murmured.

'I know. We'd better make the most of it.'

He turned towards her, tipped her mouth up to his and kissed her tenderly. It was ages before he lifted his head, and she made a small sound of protest.

'Hussy,' he murmured, and she laughed.

'It's your fault. You shouldn't be so good at it.'

'Flattery will get you everywhere,' he said, and kissed her again, then pulled her to her feet and walked her home.

They paused on her doorstep, and she turned to him, still worried. 'He will be all right, won't he? The police won't send him back again?'

He shrugged. 'Talk to the social worker in the

morning. I hope not. It doesn't sound a frightfully healthy idea.' He stooped and kissed her, and she let herself rest against the solid warmth of his body for a moment.

'Go on, you're pooped,' he murmured, and kissed the top of her head. She watched him go from the doorway, then went in. Lucy and Beth had gone to bed, and she followed suit and lay there wondering how a boy like that could survive outside in the cold and wind and rain.

She imagined him, and others like him, huddled in doorways and underpasses, under bridges and in nasty little alleyways, constant prey to the seedy, slimy dregs of humanity that stalked the night and took advantage of their fear and innocence.

And that was better than being at home?

He was looking better in the morning, warm and rested and a little less afraid. He smiled at Allie, talked guardedly to the social worker and still refused to give anyone his real name or his parents' address, although he told the social worker about his stepfather.

'If I promise that you won't have to go home to them, will you talk to the police?' the social worker asked.

'Not about that. About who beat me up in the park, yeah. I don't know who it was. I've said that.'

'Can you tell them? They need to put their files straight.'

He looked hunted, and Allie intervened. 'I'm sure there's time for that,' she said soothingly.

The social worker nodded. 'Oh, yes, there's no hurry. If you really don't know anything about it, there isn't a lot they can do anyway. Now, I understand you have to stay in hospital for a while until they're happy with your condition, is that right?'

'That's right,' Allie said.

'So if you'd only tell me who you are, I could contact Social Services in Glasgow and talk to your parents.'

'Who said anything about Glasgow?' Jimmy said sharply.

'Your accent gives you away, Jimmy,' the social worker told him. 'Nobody told me anything.'

He refused, though, and in the end the social worker gave up. 'You'll have to be made a ward of court as you're a minor.'

'How do you know? I could be sixteen.'

'Are you?'

'I might be. I don't know.'

'Well, until you do, I think it's best. It will help us to protect you better.'

He didn't look convinced, and later that day another policeman came, a detective sergeant with more clout than Dave, and started throwing his weight around. Jimmy was up and dressed and in the playroom resting in front of the television, and Allie had a confrontation with the police officer in the ward.

'I can't tell you what I don't know, and I can't tell you what I've been told in confidence,' she said firmly.

'Even if it means he's in danger?'

'He's in no danger here.'

'He might be. Without knowing who beat him up or why, you have no idea. A child of that age belongs with his family.'

'Not if his family are harming him,' she retorted.

'I'm sorry, there's nothing I can tell you, and I don't want you upsetting him and bullying him at the moment. He's in a very fragile state.'

'He needs care.'

'He's getting care. He's fine.'

'He'll run off.'

'No,' she said emphatically. 'He promised me he wouldn't—and I promised him I'd protect him.'

The policeman stabbed his hand through his hair and sighed harshly. 'I'm on his side, for heaven's sake! I want to help him.'

'Then leave him alone for a while and let him feel safe. We've got beds at the moment. We can keep him for a few days. Social Services are looking after him. Please give him time.'

'OK. But not long. Another twenty-four hours, maybe.'

Allie sighed. 'Thanks.'

He went, and she found Jimmy in the playroom, a fixed expression on his face. 'What did he want?'

'To talk to you. I've sent him away. I shouldn't really do that, Jimmy. He wants to help you.'

'He can't.'

Allie didn't know any more. She went off duty, worried about him, and it seemed she was right to be concerned, because the following morning when she arrived at work he was gone.

CHAPTER NINE

SHE worried about Jimmy all that week at work. He haunted her sleep, he invaded her thoughts when she was awake, and by the weekend she was resigned to the fact that he was probably far away and she'd never see him or hear about him again.

Mark had been wonderful, especially when the police had tried to blame her for his disappearance.

'I never did know his real name,' she'd told them. 'There was nothing to tell you that would have made any difference. I had to respect his confidence. It's part of my job.'

They'd reluctantly agreed, in the end, and she'd left them and Social Services trying to tidy up their files. Pity about them, she thought, much more concerned for Jimmy.

The weekend arrived, and Mark rang on Saturday morning announcing that he was going to move into his house that day.

'I've got everything I need now—a cooker, a kettle, working hot water, a bed—it's wonderful, and if I'm driving backwards and forwards every day to feed the cat, I might as well be here.'

'What about curtains?'

'I've bought some ready-made cream ones for now. They do the job. Come and see.'

So she went, and it was lovely. She looked upstairs in the bedroom, and there was the bed, the mattress and base making the top quite high but giving it a certain old-fashioned look. The new curtains were hung on poles, and were simple and effective, and Minnie was curled up on the new mattress ignoring them, utterly content.

'What do you think?'

'Very different,' she said with a laugh. 'I wouldn't have recognised it. Have you got bed linen?'

'Yes—want to help me make it? I washed it, because it felt a bit crunchy in the packet. It's here.'

It was cream, eyelet lace and embroidery, surprisingly feminine and yet absolutely right for the room. The quilt was new, thick and soft and filled with down, and it felt gorgeous. They evicted the disgruntled cat, put the mattress cover and sheet on, then she helped him straighten the quilt onto the bed, smoothed the cover and then met his eyes across it. They locked and held.

'You could help me christen it,' he said softly, and her heart crashed against her ribs.

She didn't speak. She didn't know what to say, apart from yes, which seemed a bit forward, absurdly.

'Tonight,' he went on, his eyes still locked with hers. 'Come for dinner. Go home now and get ready, and I'll go shopping and cook us a meal—and then stay with me, Allie. Let me make love to you.'

She dragged in a breath, then another one. 'All right,' she said, and her voice was taut and thready. 'What time?'

'Seven? Seven-thirty?'

'OK.'

They stood there, transfixed, and then she pulled herself together and moved towards the door. He stopped her, kissing her just lightly on the lips. He was shaking, his hands trembling against her wrists, and she realised he was as tense as she was.

'I'll see you later,' she murmured, and turning, she ran down the stairs, grabbed her bag and keys and let herself out. It was lunchtime. She had all afternoon to get ready, and she intended to use it.

She dug out all the smellies she'd never used, and put handfuls of stuff in the bath. After a long soak, she rinsed herself with the shower hose, washed her hair and dried herself, painted her nails, and then opened the wardrobe and wailed.

'What?' Beth asked, drifting past.

'I'm going for dinner with Mark to his cottage.'

'Oh. Nice. What are you wearing—or is that what the wail was about?'

'That's what the wail was about. I don't know what to wear, I haven't got the slightest idea.'

Beth flicked dismissively through her wardrobe, rolled her eyes and went out. 'Come on. I must have something better than that. You need to get out more, Allie.'

She followed Beth, shook her head at a few things and then took the dress. It was simple, made of heavy cotton jersey and probably not quite warm enough really for this time of year, but she could wear a cardigan over it. She had a pretty one that would do, and it was a lovely dress. Long, button through, as elegant as you made it, and comfortable. It was Beth's favourite dress, and Allie had always liked it.

'Go on, borrow it,' Beth said, resigned. 'Anything to get you out more.'

She kissed Allie on the cheek, to her surprise, and she went into her bedroom and put the dress on. It was lovely, and Beth snorted.

'Darn. It looks better on you than it ever did on me. Have it.'

'But it's your favourite!'

'I've worn it to death. Have it. I'll never wear it again, you've ruined it for me. Have it with my love.'

'Thanks.'

She twirled in front of the mirror, smiled to herself and put the cardigan on.

'That's lovely. Makes it homely—dresses it down a bit. Excellent. Cup of tea?'

Allie glanced at her watch, and found it was nearly half past six.

'No, I have to go,' she said, and nerves suddenly clamoured at her. 'Um—don't wait up for me. I won't be back.'

Beth was very still. 'Right. OK. We'll see you when we see you.'

'No smart remarks?' Allie said, her voice shaking slightly.

'Take care. Have fun. Be sensible.' She went out and came back, handing Allie a packet. 'Just in case he forgot.'

She looked down, and colour swept over her cheeks. 'Oh. Thanks.' She pushed the packet into her bag, zipped it up and smiled at Beth. 'Thanks for everything—especially the dress.'

'You look lovely. Go and wow him.'

Wow him? Huh! She was terrified, the drive seemed interminable and she was there hopelessly early. She contemplated sitting in the car, but decided that was silly. She'd help him cook or something.

She walked up the path, setting off the security lights, and knocked on the door.

'Coming—hang on.'

She heard his footsteps on the stairs, then the door swung open and he drew her in. 'You're early.'

'I know—I'm sorry. I thought of waiting outside—'

'Don't be daft. Come in.' He took her coat, and then ran his eyes up and down her and swallowed. 'You look beautiful,' he murmured.

Her breath jammed again, and she gave a little laugh to shift it. 'It's nothing special, I just washed.'

He smiled and shoved his hands into his pockets. He wasn't wearing jeans for a change, but casual trousers and an open-necked shirt in a silky, sand-washed type of fabric. It looked very touchable, and her fingers itched to stroke it.

'Um—the meal's not quite ready,' he said, his voice a little strained. 'It'll be a few more minutes. Can I get you a drink?'

'Thanks. Anything—whatever you're having.'

'White wine. Come into the kitchen.'

She followed him and took the glass he handed her. 'Smells good in here.'

'It's a chicken dish. It's all I can cook. It's a casserole.'

'It smells lovely.'

Their eyes locked, and Allie thought the tension was going to kill her. He moved first, putting his glass down and ramming his hands back into his pockets. 'Are you really hungry?' he asked, and his voice was gruff and raw and made her body shiver.

'No.'

'I promised myself I wasn't going to do this. I was going to feed you, and talk, and be civilised, but I need you, Allie, and I don't think I can wait any more.'

She closed her eyes, desire pouring through her like a rip-tide. Her chest was heaving, her heart was pounding against her ribs and she thought she was going to pass out. She felt his hand against hers, taking the glass from her just before she shattered it, setting it down on the table.

'Come to bed,' he murmured, and she opened her eyes and met his burning gaze.

'Yes,' she said, and her voice was sure and strong. He took her hand and led her up the stairs, and in the doorway he made her wait. She heard him strike a match, and then he turned out the lights and let her in.

Candles flickered on the beam over the chimney breast, fat white church candles that cast a soft yellow light over the pretty room. It was beautiful and romantic and made her want to cry.

'It's lovely,' she said softly. 'Thank you.'

He smiled, his mouth curving on one side, the rest of his face motionless. 'It's an appropriate setting for you,' he told her, his fingers easing the cardigan over her shoulders and dropping it to the ground. Then he started on the buttons, one by one, still not touching her. It was unbearably arousing, and she thought her knees would buckle.

The dress followed the cardigan, and his eyes trailed over her, leaving rivers of heat in their wake. He sucked his breath in sharply. 'Oh, Allie...'

'Your turn,' she said, and tried with trembling fingers to undo the buckle on his belt.

'Let me,' he grunted, and ripped the belt off. The trousers followed, then the shirt, hauled over his head so his hair was ruffled.

She smoothed it with her trembling fingers, and he

turned his head into her palm and laid a hot, moist kiss against the sensitive skin.

'Tell me what you want—what you like,' he said gruffly.

She gave a tiny shrug, her nerves like bowstrings. 'I don't know. We'll have to play it by ear—I've never done this before.'

He froze, and for a moment she thought he was going to stop, but then he met her eyes and his blazed with some emotion too fierce for her to deal with.

'Dear God, Allie,' he whispered. 'Never?'

She shook her head, and he swallowed hard and looked away.

'Please don't stop,' she pleaded.

'Don't worry, I won't,' he assured her rawly. 'Just give me a moment.'

He dragged a hand over his face, his expression agonised, then he took her hands in his and drew her into his arms. 'Do you have any idea how nervous I am now?' he asked.

'Why are *you* nervous? It's not your first time, surely.'

'Because it's yours. Because if I foul up—'

'What? I don't want you to perform,' she said tenderly. 'I just want you to hold me. I want to be part of you. I want to feel your body in mine.'

He shuddered, and suddenly she felt confident, sure and certain of what she was doing. Nature was very clever—it couldn't be that complicated. She reached up and drew his face down to hers.

'Make love to me, Mark,' she said softly. 'Take me to bed and hold me, and touch me, and be part of me.'

With a ragged groan he lifted her against his chest

and carried her to the bed, throwing back the quilt. He laid her on the cool, fresh sheets and followed her down, taking her in his arms at last. Their mouths locked, their bodies arched against each other and Allie thought she'd die if she had to wait any longer.

'Please,' she begged, and he stripped away the last few remnants of their clothes and threw them aside.

'Hang on,' he said tightly, and turned away, rummaging in the top drawer of the chest of drawers she'd polished so lovingly. 'Damn, my hands are shaking so much I can hardly do this,' he muttered, and then he turned back and settled gently over her.

He kissed her again, then lifted his head and stared down into her eyes. She looked up at him, so male, so powerful above her. It felt wonderful, so absolutely right she ached for him. 'Mark—'

'Are you sure, Allie?' he said raggedly, and she knew then, if she hadn't known it before, how much she loved him.

'Yes, I'm sure,' she promised, and then she felt the incredible fullness of his possession and sobbed aloud.

'Oh, yes,' she whispered. 'Oh, Mark, yes... Please.'

He moved against her, his body taut and trembling under her hands, and then suddenly her body tightened.

She sobbed his name, weeping as the waves of passion washed over her, and she felt him stiffen and arch against her, crying out as the heavy pulsing beat of his climax drove her even higher and then died away, leaving them spent and helpless in its aftermath.

Then he lifted his head and stared down into her

eyes, and his lashes were clumped with tears. 'I love you,' he said softly, and she held him close and ran her hands down the smooth column of his spine and thought nothing had ever felt so right...

They ate the casserole at midnight, when hunger drove them out of bed, and then made love again on the floor in front of the fire, on a big fluffy rug that made her skin itch.

Mark laughed and pulled her to her feet. 'Let's go back to bed,' he suggested, and towed her up the stairs and into the bedroom. The candles had burned right down, and he put them out and snuggled up to her in the dark and held her close.

That was how they were lying when she woke to the sound of the church bells, her head on his chest, her arm round his waist, their legs tangled. She moved her head and his eyes opened.

'Your new bed's got roll-together,' she told him with a smile, and he laughed.

'No, I think that's us. Maybe roll-together is nothing to do with why people had so many babies. Maybe they just liked it.'

He yawned and stretched, his body like a big cat's, long and lean and graceful, the muscles rippling under the skin. She wanted to make love to him again, but her body was unused to it and she felt tender.

'OK?' he asked, and she nodded.

'Wonderful.'

'Good. How about breakfast?'

She propped herself up on one elbow and studied him. 'Are you asking me if I want it, or suggesting I get it?'

He laughed. 'Is it worth a try?'

'No.'

'I thought not.' He threw the quilt off and stood up, stretching again and treating her to a wonderful view of his naked body. She rolled onto her stomach and admired him, and he laughed at her and kissed her nose and told her not to be so impertinent.

'Put your dressing gown on and come down—we'll have breakfast in the bath.'

'The *bath*!'

He looked back over his shoulder. 'Why not?'

She shrugged and smiled. 'No reason. Good idea.'

She got out of bed, a little self-conscious in the cold light of day, and pulled her dressing gown on quickly. He watched her, his eyes darkening with intent, and she followed him downstairs.

'Run the bath and get in it—I'll bring the breakfast things,' he said.

It was actually a huge bath, she realised, and she filled it as full as the hot water would allow. He brought the tray on a little table, set it beside the bath, shucked off his dressing gown and climbed in opposite her. Their legs tangled, and he slid his feet around her hips and smiled.

'OK?'

She nodded and wondered what would happen if she dropped her toast in the water. It was all right, she didn't, but the feel of his hairy legs against her smooth ones was enough to distract her utterly.

She sipped her tea, ate another piece of toast and felt hugely contented.

Till he picked up the soap and washed her lovingly all over...

He lit the fire again once they were dressed and they curled up on his second-hand sofa and stared into the flames and sipped fresh coffee. It was lovely, she thought—so romantic and comfortable and idle.

'I could stay here for ever,' she mumbled lazily.

He put his mug down and turned to her. 'Could you?'

She looked at him, his face strangely intent, and set her own mug down warily. 'It was just an expression—'

'But would you? Would you stay here with me, make a life with me?' He took her hand in his and looked at her with unguarded eyes. 'Will you marry me, Allie? Have my children? Grow old with me?'

She just stared at him, stunned that things had suddenly gone so far without her permission—without her realising what was going on, the way he felt, what they were leading up to.

Guilt clawed at her—guilt and grief, because she suddenly realised that she wanted what he offered more than she could have believed possible.

'I—I can't,' she said, and his eyes registered confusion.

'Can't? What do you mean, you can't?'

'I can't marry you.'

'But—why? Don't tell me you don't love me—not after last night. I just won't believe you.'

'I didn't say I didn't love you,' she said wretchedly, 'just that I can't marry you. You know that. You must understand.'

'Understand?' he said, very softly. 'No, I don't understand. Not after last night. Not after you gave me your virginity, for God's sake! What is there to understand?'

His words lashed her, flaying her with her own guilt.

'I'm sorry,' she mumbled. 'I didn't realise you felt the way you do. I didn't want to hurt you, Mark—I didn't want to hurt either of us. I thought we could have an affair, enjoy each other, have some fun—'

'Fun? Is that what you call what we did last night? Having *fun*? Allie, I gave you my soul last night. Didn't you even *notice*?'

A sob rose in her throat, and she bit her lips to stop the sound emerging. 'I'm sorry,' she whispered, her heart in shreds. 'I didn't mean to hurt you—'

'For God's sake, woman, just tell me why!'

She stared up at him, towering over her, his face ravaged by grief and anger. 'I have told you. I've told you over and over, but you wouldn't listen. Mark, you're going to be a GP—'

'And that's it? That's all it takes to stop you? My career choice? I'm sorry,' he said savagely, 'I didn't think being a GP was so bad you wouldn't marry me over it!'

'Remember Robert?' she said in an anguished voice. 'Remember his wife, torn with grief, his little children deprived of their father because the stress was just too much? It happens all the time, Mark! It's not just Robert who can't cope. Lots of GPs can't cope, and they kill themselves. I don't want to be a widow, Mark, and I don't want to wait all my life for the day the police come round to tell me you've taken an overdose or gassed yourself in your car! I can't live like that, Mark, and I won't. I'm sorry.'

'You really mean it, don't you?' he said heavily, and sat down suddenly as if his strings had been cut. 'My God. I thought we had it all, Allie. I thought we had roses round the door and happy ever after, and all we had was a lie.'

'No. Not a lie,' she said brokenly. 'I love you. You know that.'

'And I'm going to be a GP. You know that— you've known it all this time, Allie. I haven't made any secret of it. It's what I am. I'm just a family doctor. That's all I've wanted for years. I just look a long time to realise it, but now I know, it's the path I have to follow. Just like you and your nursing. It's who I am, Allie, and I can't live a lie. I have to be true to myself, even if it means losing you, because if I'm not true to myself, I'm nothing—'

His voice broke and he stood up, crossing to the window. The churchgoers had all gone home, the lane was quiet. 'Your parents are happy,' he said, trying to reason with her. 'Your father's a GP.'

'Yes. He's constantly tired, he works horrendous hours, he's under huge diagnostic pressure, he has to be an expert in every disease—that's just the job. But then it affects their private life, too. They never eat together at night, they can never go anywhere because he gets called out—even when he's not on call he goes out—'

'But that's his choice, Allie.'

'And my mother hates it. She's had to sacrifice her life for him, and there have been times I thought their marriage wouldn't survive. Well, I won't do it, Mark. I can't. Don't ask me to.'

'Maybe she thought the sacrifice was worthwhile,' he said softly.

'Maybe. That's her choice. This is mine. I'm sorry. I do love you, but I can't marry you, Mark, and if that's the end for us, well, that's how it has to be.'

He turned as she stood up, and his face was drained of emotion. All except his eyes, and in his eyes was a pain she hoped she'd never see again.

'That's how it has to be,' he said quietly. 'Take your things with you and shut the door behind you when you go.'

He picked up his coat, slung it over one shoulder, pocketed his keys and went out, leaving the door wide open. She watched him walk away, his dignity the only thing holding him together, and her heart shattered.

She gathered her things together mechanically, put them in the car and then went back inside the cottage, looking round it with dry, wounded eyes. She loved it. She loved him. She hadn't known anything could hurt so much.

Closing the door behind her was like closing the door on her heart...

CHAPTER TEN

WHY was it, Mark thought, stabbing viciously at the preset buttons on his car radio, that whenever you wanted cheering up they played mournful love songs?

He tuned to another station, and hit the 'off' button in disgust a minute later. The very last thing he needed was Patsy Cline's 'Crazy' or Elvis Presley singing 'Love Me Tender'!

He gave up. Silence was preferable, punctuated by short, harsh sighs of regret.

He sighed again, swallowing the emotion that rose up to choke him out of the blue. That was the worst thing, he realised, not knowing when it was going to hit you. He'd got through the night, more or less, waking at four to huge, racking sobs that had come from nowhere.

He'd got up and made a cup of tea, and found a glass with her lipstick on it by the sink. He'd picked it up and hurled it across the room, but it hadn't helped, any more than the glass of Scotch or the aspirin or the soothing bath he'd had before he went to bed.

Nothing helped. It just needed time—about a hundred years should do it. He'd gone back to bed, but her scent was on the sheets, soft and delicate and enough to slice right through him.

Eventually he'd slept again, a fitful sleep stalked by nightmares. He'd got up at six, gone for a run and nearly killed himself falling over a log in the half-dark, and now he was on his way to work with a scraped shin and a disposition as sour as a lemon.

He just felt gutted. Totally, utterly gutted, empty inside, scraped clean and raw and bleeding.

Anna was the first person to see him, and she gave him a sharp look and wheeled him into the office, shutting the door behind her. 'What the hell happened to you?' she asked directly, and he swallowed convulsively and looked away.

'Don't ask. Don't be nice to me, don't talk to me about anything except work.' He gulped again and took a long, steadying breath, then another one. 'Where's Allie?' he asked in a voice he didn't recognise.

'Day off. She had a long weekend. Have you had a bust-up?'

'You might call it that,' he said through gritted teeth. 'Anna, I really don't want to talk about this.'

'OK.' She scribbled something on a piece of paper and tucked it into his shirt pocket. 'Just in case you do, this is my number. Ring me or call round. I've got broad shoulders, Mark. You might want to use them.'

She walked out—no gratuitous sympathy, no pitying hug—nothing to undermine his fragile control. He was grateful for that. He had to work today—had to concentrate and do the things required of him to the best of his ability, regardless of how he might feel.

Dear God, it was going to be difficult.

Allie didn't know how she'd get through the next few days. Seeing Mark, when she eventually did on Tuesday morning, was devastating. He looked at her across the ward, his eyes silently reproachful, and turned away.

Anna found her minutes later in the sluice, sobbing her heart out over the sink.

'Oh, Allie,' she said gently, and hugged her. It made it worse, sort of, but it was wonderful to have some comfort, to feel someone's arms around her soothing her. She felt about three years old and just as confused.

'I didn't know it could hurt so much,' she said unevenly when the sobs had died away. 'I thought I'd be all right. I thought I'd get over him, but the way he looked at me—like I was some kind of murderer—'

She sniffed and rummaged for a tissue, and Anna pulled a piece off the dispenser on the wall and handed it to her. 'Here. Dry up, have a wash and come and help me with the drugs. I need to stock-check.'

She nodded, and Anna stood over her while she blew her nose and wiped her eyes and splashed her face with cold water. Then she bullied and fussed her for the rest of the day, keeping her away from Mark, chivvying her through her tasks and making sure she was so busy she didn't have time to think.

Not until she went home, that was. Then there was plenty of time to think. Too much.

Beth and Lucy were wonderful, but they thought she was mad. 'Why?' Beth said, incredulous. 'He's gorgeous, he loves you, you love him to bits—why on earth do this to yourselves?'

Because I'm scared, she thought. Scared to death that I'll lose him, and better to hurt now than later, when we've got three children depending on him and a mortgage and a house full of his handiwork to torment me with guilt while he lies cold in his grave.

Beth and Lucy wouldn't understand, so she didn't bother to discuss it with them, just ate the food they put in front of her and stared sightlessly at the television and went to bed early so she could cry in peace.

It got easier. Over the next three or four days it eased off a fraction—either that or she simply grew used to the pain. She wasn't much use at work, but Anna kept her busy doing things she couldn't mess up, and gradually it got better.

Then one day, when Anna had gone off duty at five, she came back to the ward and spoke to Mark. Allie knew this because she was watching Mark out of the corner of her eye, torturing herself with his presence.

He was about to finish, and he looked at his watch, said something to Anna and smiled, and a sharp stab of pain went right through her.

How she missed that smile.

Anna left again, and then Mark went, and it was as if the sun had set.

Despondent, she pulled herself together, reminded herself it was for the best and carried on with her work. She was on a late, finishing at nine o'clock, and by the time she handed over to the Night Sister she was exhausted.

Not so exhausted that she didn't spend the night torturing herself as to why Anna had come back and spoken to Mark, and why he'd smiled at her and then disappeared so soon afterwards.

She was on an early the next day, and dragged herself out of bed, quickly showered and dressed and headed over to the hospital. She was just turning into the car park entrance when she saw Anna getting out of Mark's car. She looked tired, and he was unshaven and looked—well, they both looked as if they'd been up all night.

Together? With each other?

Making love?

They walked side by side to the double doors, and as they went in Mark turned to Anna and hugged her, and Anna went up on tiptoe and kissed him.

No! Allie pressed her fingers to her mouth, holding back the bile that rose in her throat. No! Please no. Not Mark and Anna. Not so soon, not so easily.

Blindly she stumbled back to her flat and lost her hasty breakfast, then washed and tidied her hair.

'You have to go to work,' she told herself sternly. 'You have to face this like an adult. You don't want him any more, so you can't complain when someone else does—and you can't pick and choose someone you don't know, either. Take it on the chin, kid.'

She went back across to the hospital, through the doors and down the corridor towards the ward. Her feet were dragging, and she had to force herself, but she went onto the ward, smiled brightly at Anna and carried on with her work.

Thank goodness they were busy. Lots of pre-ops to reassure, lots of post-ops later to care for, and the long-stay monsters in casts and traction to keep under control.

The social worker was there about a child in foster care who had been admitted, and she asked Allie if she'd heard any more from Jimmy.

'No,' Allie said, ashamed that he'd been right out

of her mind in the last couple of weeks. 'I haven't heard a word. I don't imagine I will.'

'No, probably not. I do worry about them all, sleeping rough at that age. Well, any age, really. The nights are getting colder now—we're into November and it'll soon be frosty.'

Allie thought of Jimmy, bright and intelligent and driven from home by fear, and of Claudia, with all that love and support on her side. 'People ought to have to pass a test before they're allowed to have children,' she said, and the social worker laughed.

'Don't. It's my favourite hobby horse. It's too easy to get pregnant and too hard to live with stroppy children and difficult partners, but that's life for you, and we're here to pick up the pieces. Oh, well, must fly, I've got to see a new mum in Maternity—she's fifteen, poor kid. No doubt the romance has already worn off.'

No doubt, Allie thought. Fifteen and a mother. What a tragedy.

She turned, deep in thought, and went smack into a solid and very masculine frame. His hands came up and cupped her shoulders, steadying her, and for a blissful second her head rested against his chest and she was inhaling the warm, familiar scent of his body.

Then she hauled herself upright and stepped back. 'Sorry. I wasn't looking where I was going.'

'That's all right. I was coming to see you—we need to talk. Can we meet later?'

She made herself look at him, at the lines of exhaustion etched on his face, evidence of his lack of sleep last night, and she shook her head slowly.

'Oh, no. There's nothing you could possibly have

to say to me that I'd want to hear—and nothing I have to say to you. Please let me past.'

He stood for a moment, something that could have been anger flickering in the back of his eyes, and then he stepped to one side and she walked past him and out of the ward.

She didn't know how she got through the rest of the day, she was so angry with him. What had he wanted to say? Oh, by the way, Anna and I are an item— congratulate us? Not in this lifetime, buster!

She went home, changed into jeans and a thick sweater and did some housework. She only stopped when she'd nearly scrubbed the enamel off the kitchen sink, and she made herself a cup of tea, opened the fridge and slammed it in despair.

Nothing. No milk, no anything. She pulled on her coat and walked to the corner shop. She needed food—not jam sandwiches and cream crackers, but real, honest to goodness food. She loaded up her basket, paid for the goods and left the shop, striding briskly along the pavement in the dark.

Damn him and Anna! Why did he think she would be interested? Her mind tortured her with images of Mark's body, lean and muscled and sleek, tangled with Anna's—

'Stop it!' She turned the corner, and went across the dark bit between the end of the hospital car park wall and the beginning of her street.

Normally she would have crossed the road, but to-day she didn't. She just walked straight into them, head down—three youths, standing in the darkness, waiting.

'Excuse me,' she said, still not giving them a

thought, and then they jostled her. Not a lot, just enough to show her they meant business.

'Give us the bag, lady,' one of them said. 'We don't want to hurt you.'

Odd, she thought, how she didn't even feel fear. She was just angry, toweringly, furiously angry, and she lashed out at him with the heavy bag of shopping.

'No,' she yelled. 'Damn you, no!'

They circled her, knives glinting in the darkness, and she whirled round, swinging the bag with all her might. One boy fell, and she heard another swear just as an arm closed around her neck and hauled her head back, cutting off her air supply.

'Leave her alone!'

The cry came out of the darkness, and her assailant wavered for a second. It was enough. She slammed her elbow back into his ribs, and the grip slackened enough for her to scream. Then she heard footsteps running, and the shopping was torn from her hand and she was thrown to the ground.

There was a thud and a cry of pain, and then nothing but the sound of running feet as the boys fled. She opened her eyes and sat up, and saw a figure huddled on the ground a few feet away, moaning.

'Are you all right?' she asked, her voice trembling.

'Allie, it's me—Jimmy,' he groaned. 'I'm OK. Are you all right? Did they hurt you?'

'No—I just fell over.' She was about to get to her feet when she heard running footsteps. Oh, no, she thought, they're coming back, but then strong, gentle hands closed over her arms and Mark's face appeared dimly in her line of vision.

'Allie? For God's sake, Allie, tell me you're all right—'

'I'm fine.' She pulled her arms away from him and struggled to her feet, pushing him aside. 'Please—I'm all right. I don't need you.'

She heard him suck in his breath, and he stepped back, out of her way. 'I was coming to talk to you—'

'I told you, you've got nothing to say that I want to hear. If you want to talk, I suggest you talk to Anna.'

'I have. That's why—'

She covered her ears. 'I don't want to know. Get out of the way, I have to see to Jimmy.'

She elbowed past him and crouched down, laying a gentle hand on the boy's shoulder. 'Are you all right? Can you stand?'

'Don't know. My hand hurts—it feels sticky. Did he have a knife?'

'Yes.' She looked around, and Mark was still there, hands thrust into pockets. 'Help me get him to A&E—'

'No! I'm not going back in there!' Jimmy said, panic-stricken. 'The police—'

'What the hell's he doing here?' Mark said roughly. 'I thought you said you hadn't seen him again?'

'I haven't,' she snapped. 'I don't know what he's doing here, but I'm not going to complain. I think he just saved my life! Now get over here and help me with him, or go and call someone who will.'

Mark only hesitated a moment, then he was there by her side, hoisting Jimmy to his feet and helping him towards the light. They sat him down on the low wall by the car park, and Mark crouched down and sucked in his breath through his teeth. 'That needs stitches. You'll have to go into the hospital, Jimmy, I'm sorry.'

'No!'

'My father could do it,' Allie said. 'I'll drive him over there—'

'You aren't driving anywhere in your condition. You've just been mugged, for God's sake. You need to speak to the police.'

'Why? Because some hungry kids stole my shopping? I'm more worried about Jimmy.' She turned to the boy, crouching down so she was on his level. 'Will you let my father look at your hand? He's a doctor—a GP. He can stitch it for you, and he won't tell anyone about you.'

He hesitated, then nodded. 'OK.'

'My car,' Mark said. 'I'll drive you, if you insist on going.'

'I do.'

'Fine. I'll bring it.'

He was back a moment later with the car, and he put Jimmy in the back with a clean pad of gauze over the cut, and then slid behind the wheel. Allie sat beside him in a tense silence all the way to her parents' house, and then as they turned onto the drive she was out of the door and in the house, explaining to her parents as quickly as she could about Jimmy and the mugging.

'Are you all right?' they asked anxiously, and she nodded.

'I'm fine. It's Jimmy I'm worried about.'

She'd already told them all about him in the past, and as they hurried towards the door she reminded them that he hated the police.

Her father tutted gently over the hand and led

Jimmy away to the little room he sometimes used to see patients, and Allie's mother turned to Mark and gave him a warm smile. 'What a good job you were there! It might have been really nasty.'

'He came afterwards—it was Jimmy who helped me,' Allie corrected firmly.

Her mother blinked. 'Oh. Sorry. Still, Mark, it's nice to see you. Thanks for bringing them over. How are you? We haven't seen you in ages—how's the house?'

'Um—fine. I'm afraid I'm going to have to go. Allie, are you all right?'

She nodded. 'I'm just a bit shaken. Thank you for the lift.'

His mouth twisted in a bitter smile. 'My pleasure. I'll tell Anna you won't be in tomorrow.'

'You do that.'

Anna's mother gave her a strange look and put a hand on his arm. 'Mark, can't you stay for supper?'

'No,' they chorused, and then both looked away.

'I have to go. I'll see you soon.'

He let himself out, and Allie's mother turned to her with a puzzled look. 'Allie? What's going on? I thought you two were so close?'

And that was it. The floodgates opened, and she told her mother all about Mark and his proposal and how she'd ended it.

'I don't understand,' her mother said, looking confused. 'You said you love him.'

'I do love him,' she said wretchedly.

'Then—why don't you marry him?'

'Oh, Mum, didn't you hear me? He's going to be a GP!'

Her mother stared at her. 'I don't understand. Why is that a problem?'

'Why?' Allie stared back at her, equally confused. 'Think about Robert killing himself—think about Dad being so tired all the time, the awful life you've had, never being able to plan a meal or go out because of his work—'

'But that's your father. That's not the job, that's the way your father chooses to do the job. He fought tooth and nail with the other partners not to join the co-op because he wanted to do his own night calls. And yes, it's stressful, but it makes him happy, and I wouldn't want him to be anything else. I can't imagine anything worse than a man coming home discontented from a job he hates—especially if he was doing it just for me. I couldn't ask him to do that—he wouldn't be your father if he wasn't a GP.'

Allie stared at her, dumbstruck. *I can't imagine anything worse than a man coming home discontented from a job he hates—couldn't ask him to do that—doing it just for me—wouldn't be your father...*

Oh, Lord. Allie took a steadying breath and looked up. 'Mum, I'm worried about Jimmy. He's been sleeping rough for a year—he isn't safe. I don't want him back on the streets again—'

'Do Social Services know about him?'

She nodded. 'Yes. Why?'

'Well, you know we used to foster children occasionally—children like him, short-term cases awaiting trial or assessment. They might let him stay here with us while it's all sorted out. Maybe for longer, who knows?'

She nodded. 'He said once that he'd like to be a doctor. I don't know how realistic that is.'

'Well, we'll find out. I'll ring Social Services. Don't you worry about Jimmy, we'll feed him and put him to bed and he'll feel better in the morning. Then we'll talk about his future. I have to say, the house feels awfully empty without any children around now, and it might be nice to do some fostering again. I'll have to see what your father says, of course, but as he's not retiring yet—'

'He's not stopping at Christmas?' Allie said, stunned.

'No. He's changed his mind. I knew he would. He was just tired. He's cut his time back to three-quarters, but he's not going to give up. I don't think he can. He's not like that. He loves it too much.'

Allie stared at her mother, her earlier words echoing in her head again. *I can't imagine anything worse than a man coming home discontented from a job he hates—especially if he was doing it just for me. I couldn't ask him to do that—he wouldn't be your father if he wasn't a GP.*

Was that what she'd asked of Mark? That he should be someone different? Someone other than the man she loved? Did she really want him discontented and miserable because he was doing a job he hated?

'What about Robert?' she said. 'He didn't love it.'

'No, he didn't. He shouldn't have gone into medicine at all, he should have followed his heart and been a solicitor—that was what he wanted to do, but his father wanted him to follow in his footsteps.'

'Dad wanted *me* to do the same.'

'Because he thought it was what you wanted. When you said you didn't, he was quite happy for you to choose your own path in life. Robert's father wouldn't pay his way through college if he didn't go into med-

icine, and he pushed his son into suicide in the end.
Your father would never have done that to you.'

'You never told me any of this. All this time I
thought he killed himself just because of the pressure.'

'And that's why you won't marry Mark? Because
you don't want him in a job with so much pressure?
What about hospital medicine, Allie? That can be horrendous, too—worse in some cases. There isn't an
easy branch of medicine if you aren't cut out for it—
and if you are, there's nothing else you can imagine
yourself doing. And I think your Mark is one of the
latter.'

Allie swallowed. 'He spent last night with Anna,'
she blurted out.

Her mother sighed and patted her hand. 'Oh, darling, I'm sorry—but are you sure it was like that? And
even if it was, are you sure it matters? Does he love
Anna? Or was it comfort?'

She shook her head miserably. 'I don't know. I just
know I love him and I've always loved him and I
don't know what I'll do without him.'

'Then why don't you go and tell him that?'

She gave a hollow laugh. 'Because I don't have a
car here?'

'I'll run you back. It won't take long. Your father
can talk to young Jimmy and find out a bit more about
him and what he wants from life.'

'There we are—all done,' her father said, coming
into the room with Jimmy in tow, all cleaned up and
stitched. 'Allow me to introduce you to Alastair
Munro. He's going to stay here for a little while and
rest.'

Jimmy gave her a bashful smile. 'Your dad wormed it out of me.'

'Did he? He's good at that. So's Mum. You be good to them, now—and no bunking off!'

He shook his head. 'I won't. Your dad says the police won't take me away because they can foster me—for a bit, anyway.'

Her parents exchanged smiles of understanding, and Allie realised how very much they loved each other. That was how she felt about Mark—would she have a lifetime to show it, or had she thrown away her only chance of happiness?

'Now, young lady, how about you?' her father asked. 'Are you all right?'

She smiled at him ruefully. 'I will be—once I speak to Mark. Can you lend me Mum to drive me home?'

He smiled back. 'Borrow her car. She doesn't need it for the next day or so. You can bring it back when you're ready, and it's insured for any driver.'

He handed her the keys from their resting place on top of the fridge, and she kissed them both goodbye, then ruffled Jimmy's hair and gave him a fleeting hug. 'Thanks for saving my life,' she said, choked once again.

'Didn't really do much,' he said awkwardly, giving her an embarrassed smile.

'You gave me a chance to get away from the man who was holding me, and I'm very grateful.' She looked up and smiled.

'I have to go. I'll ring you later.'

'Good luck,' her mother murmured.

Her father looked puzzled, but she left her mother to explain. She had enough explaining to do if she could find Mark and make him listen. After the way she'd spoken to him earlier, she had no great hopes that he would.

She drove to the hospital first, but his car wasn't there. Anna's?

She didn't want to look for him there. The cottage, perhaps. Yes, that was most likely.

She pulled up outside, relieved to see his car and that the lights were on in the sitting room. She got out of the car and locked it, and walked up the path, wiping her suddenly clammy palms on her legs to dry them.

Her heart was in her mouth, her lungs felt crushed and any minute now she thought she was going to pass out. She paused, drawing breath and gathering her nerve, and then she took the last few strides, triggering the security lights, and knocked on the door.

He opened it almost instantly, and stood unmoving in the doorway, his face a mask.

'Um—is it inconvenient?' she asked unsteadily. 'Only I wanted to talk to you. I know you probably don't want to talk to me, after what I said before, but I need to say something. I need to ask you something. I don't care that you spent the night with Anna. That doesn't matter. It's the future that worries me—the rest of our lives—and I can't live without you,' she added softly.

For a moment she thought he was going to close the door, but he was just moving, coming towards her, pulling her inside.

'Oh, my love,' he whispered, folding her against his chest and crushing her to him, rocking her against his big, familiar frame. 'I thought I'd lost you. I saw those boys running away and I thought you were

dead, and I was just coming to see you to tell you
something really important—'

'I tried to send you away.'

'I know. But I think you ought to hear it.' He let
her go, standing a few feet away, hands rammed in
his pockets as he did when he was worried about
something. 'There's a job in A&E. It's not really my
thing, but it's all I'm qualified for with my odds and
ends of rotations. In fact I'm ideally qualified for it,
and I've spoken to Ryan O'Connor and he seemed to
be in favour of me applying—'

'A&E? Why would you want to apply for that?'
she asked stupidly. 'You want to be a GP.'

'Not as much as I want to be married to you and
live with you for the rest of my life and bring up our
children with you—'

'But you'd be miserable!'

He laughed without humour. 'Allie, I'm miserable
now. I can't live without you. My job comes a very
poor second compared to my love for you—'

'But if you could be a GP and have me?'

He lifted his head and looked at her in puzzlement.
'I thought you hated the idea?'

'I did. I misunderstood completely. I've been
speaking to my parents—I hadn't told them we'd split
up, I didn't know how to. I tried to explain to my
mother, and when I put it into words she told me how
she felt about my father and who he is and what he
does, and how she couldn't ask him to do anything
else because he wouldn't be himself, and suddenly it
all made perfect sense. I can't ask you to do anything
else because you wouldn't be you, and it's you I
love.'

'Still?'

She nodded. 'Still.'

'About Anna—'

'I don't want to know.'

'Yes, you do. We sat and talked for hours. Her car had broken down, and I drove her home and stayed for supper, and then we started talking, and the next thing was it was three in the morning and I'd fallen asleep and she covered me with a blanket and left me. We did nothing, Allie. Believe me.'

She looked into his eyes, reading the sincerity in them, and smiled, relief flooding through her. 'I believe you, but it wouldn't have made any difference if you'd slept with her. I still would have wanted you back, because I know you love me and not her—'

'I'd never do that to you,' he vowed. 'I will never do that to you, as long as we live. I want you here beside me, sharing our lives, bringing up our children, struggling with the decorating and weeding the garden at the weekends, building an extension—'

'You want a skivvy,' she teased.

'I want a wife,' he corrected, standing in front of her and taking her hands. His thumbs chafed her wrists absently, tenderly. 'I want *you*. Will you marry me, Allie? Even though I'm only going to be just a family doctor? Will you marry me, and share our future—whatever it is and wherever it takes us?'

'Oh, yes,' she said softly, and he swept her up in his arms, hugging her hard against his chest, his head pressed close to hers.

'Oh, yes,' she said again. 'Whatever it is, and wherever it takes us. I love you.'

MILLS & BOON®

Makes any time special™

Mills & Boon publish 29 new titles every month. Select from...

Modern Romance™   Tender Romance™

Sensual Romance™

Medical Romance™ Historical Romance™

MAT2

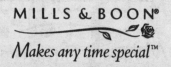

4 FREE

books and a surprise gift!

We would like to take this opportunity to thank you for reading this Mills & Boon® book by offering you the chance to take FOUR more specially selected titles from the Medical Romance™ series absolutely FREE! We're also making this offer to introduce you to the benefits of the Reader Service™—

★ FREE home delivery
★ FREE gifts and competitions
★ FREE monthly Newsletter
★ Exclusive Reader Service discounts
★ Books available before they're in the shops

Accepting these FREE books and gift places you under no obligation to buy, you may cancel at any time, even after receiving your free shipment. Simply complete your details below and return the entire page to the address below. *You don't even need a stamp!*

YES! Please send me 4 free Medical Romance books and a surprise gift. I understand that unless you hear from me, I will receive 6 superb new titles every month for just £2.40 each, postage and packing free. I am under no obligation to purchase any books and may cancel my subscription at any time. The free books and gift will be mine to keep in any case.

M0ZEA

Ms/Mrs/Miss/Mr ....Initials....................................
BLOCK CAPITALS PLEASE

Surname ....

Address ....

....

....Postcode................................

Send this whole page to:
UK: FREEPOST CN81, Croydon, CR9 3WZ
EIRE: PO Box 4546, Kilcock, County Kildare (stamp required)

From new author

Nell Brien

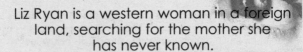

Liz Ryan is a western woman in a foreign
land, searching for the mother she
has never known.

In a culture so alien, can she
hope to succeed?

Among a people in turmoil,
can she survive?

Embark on the adventure in

A veiled journey

MIRA®   **Published 22nd September 2000**   M192